Snow and the Seven Brothers' Circus

MEGAN MILES

To my sister, Brooke
Our playtime as children taught me imagination.
Your support now encourages me to never stop dreaming.

CHAPTER 1

*E*ven thirty feet above the earth, the energy thrumming through the tent swelled to ignite the anticipation in Snow's chest. The cheers of the crowd drowned out the ringmaster's booming words, and performers decked in a dazzling array of colors and fabrics exited the ring to allow full attention on the aerial act. Before she could steal a peek at the crowd, the swinging spotlights blinded her from seeing anything below, but Snow didn't need to see them to feel the weight of a thousand eyes on her.

Squaring her shoulders, Snow turned her focus onto the only attention she needed for the next few minutes. He waited for her across the expanse, his smile beckoning her to leave the platform and fly.

And she did.

As every muscle strained to arch her body through the air, the repetitious music from the bandstand below matched the beat of her racing heart. Halfway across the dizzying void, Snow released her fingers from the trapeze bar. For a brief, heart-stopping moment, she felt nothing but the electric energy around her.

Then strong hands wrapped around her wrists, anchoring her to safety once more, and she looked up into a smile that made everything else fade away. Riding on the rising roar of the crowd, Snow swung in the security of his grasp. Transferring from his hands by hooking her legs over the waiting bar, thrill carried her into the next death-defying move with no regard for aching muscles or tiring stamina.

Every fiber of her being glided on the wings of euphoria.

~

JULY 1910

Catherine's eyes flickered open, her ears ringing with cheers from a fading dream, but as the colorful image faded, the dull darkness of her room settled over her. Her wardrobe, vanity, and bookcases stood around the perimeter of the room like sentinels gazing down on her prone position. The stillness of the air gave the large room an empty feeling, like a body with no soul, and the silence left a hum in her ears.

Catherine tried to shift on the mattress, but the soft filling enveloped her body with an unrelenting hold. Heaviness weighed her limbs, pinning her small frame down.

Her gaze drifted to the gray curtains over the two ceiling-high windows. A small strip of sunlight peeked out from under the hem of the curtain, beckoning her to rise and welcome in the beautiful new day. As Catherine stared at the glimpse of light, something stirred in her weary spirit, bidding her to rise from the bed and throw open the curtain, but her muscles had given up before the day had even begun.

A soft knock drew her attention away from the window. Without a response from Catherine, a maid opened the door and slipped into the dark, cavernous bedroom. Clutching a tray of food to the white apron that protected her simple black dress, the maid drew near to the large poster bed with hesitant steps. Catherine frowned when the girl came close enough for her to see that she wasn't the same maid who'd tended her the day before.

"I-I'm here to deliver your breakfast, ma'am." The girl's quivering voice broke the silence.

She avoided Catherine's gaze as she held the tray up, featuring a meager assortment of bland food. Toast with barely enough butter to soften the dark brown surface. A single hard-boiled egg. A small bowl of chunky applesauce.

"Thank you." Catherine's husky voice sounded strange to her own ears. She tried to push herself upright, but her arms shook from the effort. Before she could get far, the maid set the tray at the foot of the bed and hurried to her side. The maid couldn't have been any older than her own twenty years, but Catherine felt like an ancient crone as the girl supported her back with one arm and drew her pillows up with the other.

"Thank you," Catherine echoed her previous phrase as she sank into the pillows again and pulled her frizzy black braid over her shoulder.

The maid offered a fleeting smile before fetching the tray from the foot of the bed. With tenderness and care, as if she was afraid one wrong touch may harm Catherine, she settled the tray on Catherine's lap and assisted her in unfolding the napkin to drape over her cream nightgown.

Folding her hands politely in front of her, the maid drew back two steps. "Is there anything else I can assist you with? Perhaps some light while you eat?"

Catherine motioned to her covered windows. "I'd like to see the sunlight. It must be a beautiful day."

The maid hesitated, her gaze darting to the window. Her mouth opened before she snapped it shut, and she gripped her hands together. "I... Mrs. Combs gave me strict instructions not to disturb the curtains. She told me that the sunlight wouldn't be good for your condition. She doesn't want it to drain your energy or bring about a headache."

Catherine set her jaw and stared into the applesauce on her tray. "It can't put me in any worse condition than I already am," she muttered through clenched teeth.

"P-pardon?" The maid drew one step closer and inclined her ear to listen.

Closing her eyes, Catherine flicked her wrist. "Never mind. That will be all."

The timid maid practically fled the room, and it wasn't until the door clicked shut behind her that Catherine realized she had neglected to ask for the girl's name. Maybe it was for the best. Most didn't last long enough for Catherine to make any sort of acquaintance.

She picked up the spoon to stir at the applesauce, but the sight of her own soft, bony hand soured whatever appetite she had. Dropping the spoon, she turned her palms upward. Flickering images from her memory returned, memories of strength that once coursed through her muscles. Of callouses that once marked the base of her fingers.

Catherine pushed the tray further down her lap. Tilting her head back on the pillows, she closed her eyes. She tried to conjure up the colorful, dazzling images of her dreams, but broken snippets of incomplete memories flickered behind her eyelids.

An ache filled her chest with a longing to return to the times of yesteryear, if only for a moment. To a time where she basked in the sunlight and laughed with youthful joy. Perhaps those days were short-lived themselves, but it was the one time in her life when everything felt right.

She laid still, beckoning sleep to take her under so that, at least in one form or another, she could return. As she drifted off, a smiling gaze surfaced once more in her mind, and she stretched her hand toward him.

CHAPTER 2

MAY 1904

Catherine pumped her legs as hard as she could, her gaze locked on the rail at the back of the train. To her alarm, the train began to pick up speed faster than she'd predicted, forcing her to dig deep in her muscles for more speed than she knew she had. Desperation clawed at her gasping lungs as the rail began to pull away. Somewhere in the back of her mind, a voice told her that she should stop running. Stop running and go back to what she knew, even if it felt like a living hell. The unknown before her could be far worse.

But the further the rail pulled away from her, the more Catherine realized how desperately she needed this chance. With tears blurring her vision, she let out a strangled cry and leaped, aiming her outstretched hand. The tips of her fingers brushed the cold metal as it slipped beyond the reach of her grasp, and she squeezed her eyes shut in preparation for the painful tumble onto the railroad tracks.

As her fingertips lost contact with the rail, strong hands wrapped around her wrist. Before she could open her eyes, her body was snatched through the air, and she tumbled onto the small platform. Her rescuer grunted as they both landed in a heap.

Catherine found enough sense to roll off of her rescuer, eyes still squeezed shut and lungs gasping for air.

She'd made it. A feat she'd thought impossible outside of books. She'd hopped a train.

Except she was already caught. That wasn't part of the plan. As her breath returned, Catherine dared to open her eyes to look at her rescuer. A boy somewhere near her fourteen years crouched beside her, his elbows resting on his knees as he watched her. His shining black hair fell straight over his forehead, shading his monolidded eyes. When their gazes met, he smiled, but she dropped her eyes as she pushed herself upright.

"You lost this," the boy spoke up. He held a dirty flat cap in her line of sight.

A "thank you" lodged in her throat as she took the hat back and jammed it onto her choppy haircut.

The boy stood to his feet and held out his hand to help her up, but she stared at his spindly arm, wondering how he had managed to pull her onto the train by himself. When she finally took his hand, the strength of his grasp surprised her. She staggered to her feet with his help, and once they were both standing, she realized she had a couple of inches on him.

"Welcome to the Seven Brothers' Circus," he declared as she took a step back to brush off her blue shirt and brown trousers that almost didn't reach her shoes.

Her gaze flickered to the train door, her bottom lip finding its way between her teeth.

"What's your name?" the boy persisted.

She opened her mouth, her name on the tip of her tongue, but she remembered herself in time to grunt out, "George Jones," in a voice deeper than her natural one.

He tilted his head, a smile slowly spreading over his lips. She fidgeted under his scrutiny, tugging her hat lower. Could he see the truth under her chopped hair and dirt-smudged face?

"Nice to meet you, Jones. My name's Sunny."

She raised her eyebrows at the curious name, but before she could summon the bravery to ask, he turned on the heels of his bare feet and opened the door to the train. "Follow me."

Catherine hesitated as he disappeared into the train car. At this point, she was caught. It wasn't like she could run and hide after he'd already pulled her onto the train. She had no choice but to face the consequences of her actions and hope that they weren't any worse than what she had left behind.

As Sunny led her through two train cars, she realized how easy it would have been to hide if she hadn't been caught. The cars were riddled with trunks, rolled canvases, and mysterious items draped in white sheets. If she had been a little faster, she could have hidden until the next stop.

Sunny helped Catherine hop the expanse between each car with his strong, secure grasp, but her eyes couldn't resist dipping to the racing tracks beneath them as she leapt. Fear knotted at her stomach, causing her to hold his hand a little tighter than necessary until her feet were secure again.

Light spilled out of the third car when Sunny pushed the door open. Catherine followed him inside, but she stopped in her tracks when six pairs of eyes swung to face her. Six men lounged on trunks that littered the room, their faces illuminated by the gas lights on the walls. The door fell shut against her heels as she remained rooted in place.

"We had a stowaway," Sunny declared as he hopped onto a large trunk next to one of the men. "A stowaway so eager to join up there was no regard for life or limb."

Sunny flashed her a grin riddled with crooked teeth. Instead of the anger or distrust she expected, grins rippled across the other six faces too. The man next to Sunny stood to his feet. He hooked his thumbs behind suspenders, which held up his brown wool pants, and his dark blue eyes didn't seem unkind as he appraised her. His long, dark hair was pulled behind his head, revealing streaks of gray at his temples, and his thick beard bore the same salt-and-pepper coloring.

After studying her long enough to make her cheeks burn, he shot Sunny a sideways glance. "What is your act, stowaway?"

Catherine unglued her tongue from the roof of her mouth to lick her lips. "I-I... No act, sir. I, um, I was hoping you would hire me as an extra hand." When he raised his dark eyebrows, she dropped her gaze to the floorboards. "I'm so sorry. I know hopping trains is illegal, but I'll work hard to earn my place. I'll do whatever you ask of me." She almost forgot about deepening her voice and added it into the last sentence, hoping no one else noticed. If they did, maybe they would think she was a boy whose voice had yet to change.

At first silence met her explanation, and when she dared to look up, the six men and Sunny were exchanging looks. She took advantage of their distraction to observe the eclectic group. Most of them wore simple buttoned shirts and wool pants, but one man sat on a trunk in a trim navy suit with his back straight as a rod. His brows lowered over scowling hazel eyes, his lips pressed in a line under his twirling mustache.

A tall, broad man leaned against the wall of the train, swaying with the movement of the rocking car. His gaze trailed between the others and Catherine. Even though he didn't scowl like the suited man, his impressive size alone made Catherine want to cower. His blue shirt and brown vest drew tight across his barrel chest, the arms of the shirt straining against his muscles even as his arms hung at his sides.

Two dark-skinned young men with a strong resemblance watched her with curious gazes. One of them had been lying across two trunks when she'd entered with Sunny, but now he propped himself up on his elbow, holding the flat cap that previously covered his face.

The final young man fidgeted with a handkerchief in his fingers, his gaze jumping around the group, but never going to Catherine. Every once in a while, he lifted the handkerchief to mop near the edge of his light brown hair.

After what felt like an eternity of traded looks, the first man to address Catherine dropped to one knee so that their gazes met at an even level. "What's your name, stowaway?"

"George Jones," she whispered, shrinking under his perceptive blue eyes.

His gaze flickered over her wispy frame. "Age?"

This time she forced herself to square her shoulders. She was trying to convince them to hire her, wasn't she? They wouldn't want a boy afraid of his own shadow. "Fourteen, sir. I'm small for my age, but I'm strong." Or at least, she hoped with enough time she could grow to be.

The man cut another sideways glance at Sunny. "We're well aware that everyone grows at different rates."

Sunny rolled his eyes and smiled in return. Compared to most of the men in the train car, Sunny's small frame was dwarfed, but she imagined his strength made up for his stature.

"What are you running away from, George Jones?" The man captured her attention again with his question, his tone softening.

She licked her lips again. That was a question she didn't have an answer prepared for.

"Your family?"

"No," she answered without hesitation. "I have no blood kin left on this earth. There's nothing at all left for me in Charleston." That was one bit of truth she could state without wavering, even if she delivered it under a stolen flat cap, choppy hair, and baggy boy's clothes that she prayed disguised any of her blossoming feminine figure. She knew without a shadow of a doubt that no one would care that she'd left, and she had nothing to go back for.

Silence fell over the train car again, but thankfully, it didn't last as long this time.

"There's one problem." The man drew his words out.

Catherine held her breath, preparing herself to rebut any of his doubts. She could handle any job they had. She could find strength to prove her worth. She would do *anything*.

"I don't think I can hire a girl as a stagehand."

Every shred of hope she had clung to fell in tatters around her feet. The world around her seemed to fade as her body stiffened.

The man stood to his feet and walked away.

Catherine bit her lip, steeling herself as blasted tears tried to invade her eyes. They would send her back. She couldn't go back. She wouldn't. For a brief moment, she entertained the idea of whirling on her heels and fleeing the train car, but where could she go? If she hurled herself off the train at its current speed, she risked serious injury—or worse.

The man went back to the trunk Sunny still sat on and picked up a canteen resting against it. He pulled a handkerchief from his pocket and dipped the corner into the mouth of the canteen. Catherine remained frozen in place under the weight of the other six gazes until he returned to her. None of them showed surprise at her secret unveiled. Even her best attempts had not been enough. They were never fooled by her disguise.

Kneeling again, he rested one large hand on her shoulder with a gentle pressure, and he used the rag to wipe at the dirt on her face. She couldn't stop a tear from escaping her eye as he wiped at the grime she'd used in vain to roughen her soft features. He captured the tear in the handkerchief.

"I may not be able to hire you as a stagehand, but this family could use a female presence to soften our masculine edges." He removed the last smear from her chin. "If we don't scare you off first, I'm sure we can find a place for you in our troupe."

"You-you'll let me stay?"

He sat back on his heels. "If you tell me one thing: What's your real name, George Jones?"

"Catherine." She omitted her last name, but she saw no reason why she couldn't be a Jones now.

"Well, Catherine, I'm Napoleon Thorburn, but most call me Leon. I'm the circus manager. You've already met, Sunny, our trapeze artist." He glanced over his shoulder at the boy. Sunny flashed her another impish smile. "Allow me to also introduce our ringmaster, Maximilien Aubert."

Leon gestured to the man in the suit whose intense expression didn't change, but Maximilien dipped his head in greeting.

"*Bonjour*," he murmured.

"And Gerard Rye, our tattooed strongman."

When the barrel-chested man raised his hand to his brow in a salute, she noticed the ink that covered his knuckles, the back of his hand, and disappeared into his sleeve.

"Byron Pierson is our head clown and magician."

The young man with the handkerchief offered her a tentative smile, his round cheeks splotched with a red tint.

"And last, but never least, our animal whisperer, Ambrose Taylor, and his equestrian vaulting brother, Titus."

He swept his hand to the two brothers, indicating the upright one first, and at the mention of the name Titus, the lounging brother doffed his cap.

"We'll be traveling through the night before we reach our next stop." Leon gave her shoulder a gentle squeeze. "Sunny, can you see to her needs until then?"

"Sure thing." Sunny hopped off the trunk. "You want a bunk or something to sleep in?"

Catherine rubbed her arm, her gaze skittering around the group of men again. "I don't really think I could sleep."

"Okay then. You hungry?"

When she gave a hesitant shake of her head, his seemingly permanent smile finally slipped into a frown.

"Well, when I'm on a train and can't sleep, I like to watch out the last train car. That's how I saw you running to catch up. Want to come watch with me?"

"That sounds nice," she answered softly.

Sunny snatched up her hand before she realized what he was doing, and he led her from the train car. They retraced their steps until they arrived on the same platform Catherine had made her awkward entrance on. When Sunny sat cross-legged against the train wall, facing the receding scenery, Catherine followed suit.

She toyed with a thread on the cuff of her shirt as her gaze flickered to keep up with the passing trees. Her chest tightened the longer she sat there, as if the full realization of what she'd done had finally come upon her.

Everything she once knew grew increasingly far away, and she was alone with a group of men she didn't know. When dreaming up the idea in her bed—clutching the circus poster she'd torn off a lamppost—it had all seemed rather thrilling. Now the anxiety threatened to pop her lungs under its vise grip.

"Why did you want to join the circus if you don't have an act?" Sunny's abrupt question broke into Catherine's spiraling thoughts.

"I just wanted to start a new life," Catherine whispered. "To leave the past behind and be someone completely different than who I've ever been. I feel like I've already failed."

"Why? Because we learned you're a girl?" Sunny stretched out his legs, reclining on his palms. "You may be a girl, but no one says you've got to be Catherine. We don't care who you are as long as we know what to call you. Though, to be honest, I don't think I can call you George either. You don't look like a George."

Her eyebrows scrunched. "Is... Is Sunny your real name?"

"Kind of. An Sun is my real name, but these guys started calling me Sunny a long time ago. After being ridiculed for my name all my life, I rather liked it. So that's who I am now. Sunny, trapeze artist for the Seven Brothers' Circus."

Catherine drew her knees up and hugged them to her chest. A new name. A new start. The thought loosened the bands on her lungs, allowing her to draw in another breath.

"How would you turn Catherine into a nickname?" she asked. "I don't care for Cathy."

Sunny tapped his chin. "What does your name mean?"

"My mother used to tell me it meant pure."

"Pure," he muttered under his breath.

Catherine turned different versions of her name over in her head. Cat. Rin. They were catchy, but they didn't feel right. They didn't feel like her.

"What about Snow?" Sunny broke into her thoughts.

"Snow?" she echoed slowly, as if tasting the name. It felt delicate on her tongue. Delicate but beautiful.

"In Chinese tradition, snow represents purity and innocence." He reached out to touch the back of her hand. "I think it fits."

She stared at the stark contrast of her porcelain skin against the rich color of his finger. His deep tan reminded her of how her father used to take his coffee, with the perfect amount of milk.

"Snow," she repeated.

"I like it," he declared as if it sealed the deal.

She raised her gaze to the passing scenery again, letting the nickname circle in her mind. She rather liked it too. *Snow.*

A sensation like the warmth off glowing coals spread from her core to her limbs. Was this what hope felt like?

"Welcome to the Seven Brothers' Circus, Snow." When Sunny flashed his beaming smile at her again, Catherine found her lips tugged by the pull of his contagious joy.

~

JULY 1910

Catherine steadied herself with a hand on the wall as she pulled the curtain open. Sunlight burst into her dark room, highlighting the dust particles suspended in the air. She closed her eyes to let the warmth kiss her face and stir her spirit.

With one hand on the waistband of her cotton skirt and the other on the wall, she made her way to the overstuffed seat angled to face the window. Her father's journal waited on the side table. Knowing her current surge of energy would be short-lived, she wanted to make the most of it. She had started by donning real clothes instead of her well-worn nightgown, followed up by brushing and re-braiding her hair. Once upon a time, she would have opted for a pretty chignon that resembled the way her mother used to wear her hair, but today, it seemed like too much for her easily tired arms.

Easing into the chair, Catherine cracked open the journal in her lap, drawing in a deep breath of the scent of aged leather and yellowing pages. Her muddled thoughts struggled to understand her father's scrawling, but she knew that this journal provided valuable insight into how he ran the estate, managed the accounts, and oversaw his coal mines. All things that would fall on her shoulders in exactly three months when she turned twenty-one. If she turned twenty-one.

She closed her eyes as the words swam before her eyes, and for a moment, she let her chilled appendages bask in the sunlight. Even though the doctor and her guardian kept their conversations out of her earshot, it didn't take a mind reader to know they held little hope for her recovery. That meant it was up to her to hold onto hope.

Catherine opened her eyes and stooped over the journal, determined to decipher the information her father had left behind. She didn't know how long she sat flipping through the pages before her door opened. Catherine stilled, recognizing the looming presence of her guardian without a word being said. Ethel's determined steps advanced across the room, and her shadow fell over Catherine's book as she stepped between the chair and window.

"What is this about not eating your breakfast?" Ethel demanded.

Catherine closed the journal with her finger stuck inside to bookmark her place. "I wasn't hungry this morning."

Ethel set a bowl of applesauce on the side table with a clatter. "How do you expect to regain your strength if you don't eat?" Anger snapped in Ethel's blue eyes. A tendon jumped in her slender neck as she lifted her delicate chin.

Based on the soft blue women's suit she wore, Catherine wondered if Ethel was coming or going for the day. Ethel always wore those smart-looking jackets with puff sleeves and slim floor-length skirts when she conducted what had once been Catherine's parents' business. Her blonde hair was smoothed into a bun, concealing any gray strands. The wrinkles around her eyes and pink lips belied her forty-some years of age, but they did little to decrease her ageless beauty. The woman knew how to look both formidable and alluring at once.

Catherine tried to straighten her spine to match her guardian's assertive posture. "I'm out of bed for the first time this week, aren't I? I will eat when I'm hungry."

"And what's this?" Ethel turned on her heels to yank the curtains closed. "Don't you care about your health at all? Are you trying to drain the life out of yourself?"

Catherine set the journal next to the applesauce as she stood. "I was enjoying the sunlight. It was warming me, not draining me."

"If you need warmth, have the maid kindle a fire."

"A fire in July? There's plenty of warmth outside."

"Catherine. Honestly, I hate having to go over the same things with you every day." Ethel pressed her fingers to her temple and drew in a deep breath. "I'm doing my best to care for you like your parents would have wanted, but I have the weight of the estate and the coal mines on my shoulders as well. If you could do something as simple as follow your doctor's orders, that would make things much easier."

Catherine swallowed her replies as she dropped her gaze to the rug. "Will you please fetch the maid to light my fire?" She rubbed her arms to ward off the unexplainable chill she felt to her bones.

"I suppose, but if you had the energy to get out of bed and dress, I don't see how it could be so hard to walk across your room." As if to demonstrate, Ethel strode with exaggerated steps to pull the string on the wall that rang for the maid.

"What's her name?" Catherine asked.

"Who?" Ethel snapped with an air of impatience.

"The new maid that delivered my food this morning."

Ethel narrowed her eyes as if trying to remember. "Oh, the slight new thing? Helen, I believe. Why? Did she do something wrong? Do I need to let her go? I can't seem to find any good help these days."

"No, no." Catherine waved a hand to stop her guardian's barrage of words. "I just didn't get the chance to ask."

"You rang?" The maid slipped in the door. Next to the towering figure of her guardian, the young woman looked like a frightened mouse ready to bolt.

"She needs a fire." Ethel snapped her fingers toward the fireplace.

Despite the confused expression that passed over her face, the maid jumped to do Ethel's bidding, and as she knelt by the fireplace, her skittish gaze flickered to Catherine.

Catherine offered her a small smile in return. "I was told your name is Helen?"

"I-it's actually Ruth, ma'am." Ruth's face reddened as she poked the log to encourage the sparks.

Catherine set her jaw as she glanced at her guardian, but Ethel watched the maid with a hawklike gaze.

"There you go, miss." Ruth jumped to her feet once the fire burned steadily at the wood. "Do you need anything else?"

"That will be all for now. Thank you."

The girl bobbed into a quick curtsy before fleeing the room.

Catherine leaned against the back of the chair as she stared at the fire. "Do you know anything about her family or her life?"

Ethel frowned. "Whose?"

"Ruth, the maid."

"Why would I know about a servant's personal life? Eat your applesauce, and ring for me if you want something more." She crossed the room again and picked up the journal from the side table. "Why are you reading this? It will stress you and wear you out. If you need an activity to fill your time, your trunk is stocked with embroidery supplies. You need to find less strenuous activities for your mental capacity."

"That's my father's journal." Catherine tried to protest, but Ethel had already crossed the room again. She slammed the bedroom shut behind herself as if cutting off Catherine's words.

Catherine glared into the fire, her arms crossed over her chest. Embroidery would be absolutely mind-numbing in the quiet solitude of her room, but what could she do that wouldn't bring another lecture about her stress and health?

She stood by the fire for several minutes, and as the warmth seeped to her core, the restlessness of her spirit grew too strong to ignore. Leaving behind her untouched bowl of applesauce, Catherine shuffled out to the hallway. Even if Edith wasn't around to see it, stepping into the hall felt like a declaration of her own independence. She wasn't so far gone that she had to sit in her bed and embroider.

Her stockinged steps were muffled on the long rug that stretched the length of the hall. Tall doors stood on either side of the hall, and portraits of people she didn't know stared down at her. They were all blood relatives in some form or another, perhaps some had even been previous residents at her family's home, but her parents had passed before they could teach her. The electric sconces on the walls highlighted their intimidating expressions. The lights had been the last modern convenience her father added to their home.

Catherine braced a hand on the wall to support herself until she reached the door she wanted. When she peeked in, a lone servant dusted the shelves. The delicious light of the day poured through two tall windows. The rays of sunlight seemed to spotlight the piano in the center of the room, beckoning her to sit and play.

Catherine slipped inside but left the door ajar. No need to alarm Ethel further with unscrupulous behavior by being alone with a male servant. She offered the servant—another one she didn't recognize—a smile as she advanced to the piano. "I hope it won't disturb your work if I play for a few minutes."

He bowed to her and left the room without a word.

Her heart sank at being abandoned once more, but she turned her attention to the piano. She didn't need to draw out the sheet music as she rested her fingers on the keys. The lessons drilled into her from childhood took over as she let the first notes ring out. They sounded empty in the vacant room, and she tried to ignore memories of a mother who once loved to sit and listen to her play. Those memories made the room seem emptier.

Catherine channeled all of her focus into playing the songs of her memories, even as her stiff fingers stumbled over some of the keys. She tried to play away the loneliness of being in a house full of people who never dared to talk to her. She tried to play away the memories that left an ache worse than the ones in her bones. She tried everything to forget, if only for a moment, and lose herself in the music.

Before she could finish the second song, a cramp seized her

wrist and spread to her palm. When tingles filled her fingers, Catherine stopped playing to rub her right wrist. Tears burned in her eyes as she massaged her left thumb up her wrist and into her palm, trying to chase away the cramps.

No matter what she did, she couldn't escape the reminders of her invisible wasting disease that was slowly sucking the life from her bones. As the tears spilled down her cheeks, familiar exhaustion washed over her in a wave, and she laid her head against the piano in defeat.

Even seated in the sun, a chill soaked through her clothing to intensify the aching in her bones. Catherine closed her eyes as a craving ached in her chest. A craving for the long-lost arms of a mother who loved her. A craving for the soul-warming smiles of a friend she once knew.

A craving for anyone to take notice of her before she slipped away forever.

CHAPTER 3

JUNE 1904

With a grunt, Snow adjusted the heavy wooden crate full of ropes in her arms. She slipped through a canvas flap into the big top brimming with activity. Even if it seemed like a small thing, carrying this crate across the campgrounds-turned-circus made her chest swell with pride. In one month since joining the circus, she'd proven herself capable of more than she knew she ever could. Her first days had revolved around helping mend costumes, since her one skill seemed to be holding a needle and thread, but doing that all day every day had nearly bored her to tears. In time, she had convinced Leon that he could use a female stagehand. She wanted to be around the performers, to witness the inner workings of the circus with her own eyes.

Now she knew how each of these large, striped tents went up and came down at every stop, and she could even help carry the heavy canvas. She had pulled ropes and steadied poles with her own two hands.

Snow peeked around the crate in her arms to watch where she walked through the big top. The show wouldn't start for several hours, but the tent was alive with activity. Men moved and worked in every direction, hammering together stands for the audience, assembling the main ring, and preparing props for the show. Performers gathered near the ring to practice their performances in plain training clothes instead of their eye-grabbing costumes.

"Snow!" Leon called from her left.

She tore her gaze off the hubbub to hurry in his direction. It had taken her no time to grow comfortable with her nickname, almost like she'd had it all her life.

Leon steadied a ladder against a tall pole. The safety net for the trapeze stretched from five other poles surrounding the main ring, but it sagged from a broken rope meant to be tied to this pole.

Leon took the load from her arms and set it at their feet before pulling out a long coil of rope. "Can you spot my ladder?"

Snow's eyes widened in surprise at being entrusted with such a critical task, but she nodded. After Leon ascended the first few rungs, she planted her hands on either side of the ladder, trying to steady the shaking. She pressed her weight into it so it wouldn't fall backward.

Once at the top, Leon wove the rope through the net and then around the pole. After wrapping the end around his arm and wrist, he pulled the rope with a grunt and drew the sag out of the net.

"Can't have Sunny falling through, can we?" Leon dragged his wrist across his perspiring forehead before wrapping the rope around the pole several times. "Gerard, Snow, stake this."

He tossed what remained of the rope downward, and the strongman appeared from somewhere behind Snow to catch the end.

"Get a stake from the crate," Gerard said in her direction as he used his muscular arms to pull the rope until the wood groaned.

Snow waited for Leon to descend the ladder a safe distance

before she scrambled over to the crate. She tossed a metal stake to Gerard, and he handed her the end of the rope.

"Keep this taut while I tie," Gerard commanded as he knelt.

Snow wrapped the rope around her hands and wrists the way Leon had and then leaned her body back to keep tension on the rope. As Leon fetched a mallet from the crate to drive the stake into the dry earth, her gaze snagged on Ambrose. He walked a large black horse into the center of the ring and let it walk to the extent of its long lead before he used a thin pole to urge the horse into a circle.

His brother, Titus, stood at the edge of the ring, bouncing on his toes and shaking out his arms. He wore no shirt under his red vest, and his lean muscles rippled with the movement.

The horse picked up speed until it reached a canter, and as the horse began to pass him by, Titus used his long arms to seize hold of the handles strapped to its withers, and he vaulted himself onto the mount.

Snow's attention remained transfixed as Titus transitioned from sitting on the horse to balancing on its bare back on his hands. His limbs moved in a fluid movement as he swung around the horse's back, sometimes upside down, sometimes using the handles to dip on one side or the other. It was like some sort of dance and acrobatics in one, and through it all, Ambrose kept the horse at a smooth canter around the ring.

Titus repeated the same tricks over several times, each time completing them with what looked like flawless ease. Sweat glistened on his dark skin, but his arms held steady under the weight of his body no matter how many times he pushed himself up on his hands. With an agile motion, he sprang out of a handstand and flipped his tall, slender body through the air until he landed on two feet on the ground.

As Ambrose slowed the horse to a gentle walk, the other performers offered a round of applause, and Snow lifted her hands to do the same but found them still tangled in rope. The rope tugged against her skin, and she turned to Gerard who grinned at her, teasing the rope.

"You can release it now. I'm ready to tie it off," he said.

Snow's face flamed as she untangled her hands. Gerard twisted the rope around the stake in a complicated knot that Snow couldn't follow. When he finished, Leon clapped his back.

"This tent would fall apart without your knowledge of knots, Sailor." Leon scratched his salt-and-pepper beard as his gaze traced the safety net. "And thank you for your help, Snow. I think we've earned ourselves a break. Why don't you sit and watch the practice for a bit. I'll let you know when I'm ready for our next task."

Before she could open her mouth to insist she could keep working, Leon turned away to motion across the tent.

"You're on, Sunny," Leon bellowed above the bustle.

Snow spotted Sunny near the ladder that led to the trapeze platform. He straightened from rolling his pant legs up his calves, and he saluted before he scampered upward.

"Holler when you need me," Snow said as she stepped toward a finished set of stands. Even though all of the performers were fun to watch, she could never seem to take her eyes off Sunny when he took to the trapeze.

The magic-wielding clown sat on the first bench of the stands, digging through a worn suitcase seated next to him. Like everyone else, Byron wore a plain shirt and trousers instead of his clown uniform. A bowler tilted back on his head.

Snow sat a couple of feet away from him on the same bench, and when their eyes met, she offered him a small smile that he returned. He pulled his hand out of the suitcase, his fingers fisted tight. He made a show of looking his fist over before raising it his lips. With a wiggle of his eyebrows, Byron blew into his curled fingers and jumped when a flower popped out the other end. With a tip of his hat, he extended the fabric flower to Snow. As she accepted the flower with a giggle, she noticed the tips of his ears blazing bright red.

She gave the petals an exaggerated sniff. "Why, thank you." She held the edge of her calf-length skirt and crossed her legs in a mock curtsy from her seated position.

Her attention snagged on Sunny again as he stood at the top of the thirty-foot-high trapeze platform. His fingers wrapped around the bar that would carry him across the dizzying expanse of the tent. He took a few deep breaths, bouncing on his bare toes. Perhaps it was her imagination, but his gaze seemed to connect with hers for a split second, his lips turning up at the corners. Then he pushed off from the platform and let momentum swing his body through the air.

Snow bit her lip as a smile snuck up her mouth. Unable to take her eyes off his graceful flight, she gripped the edge of the bench as Sunny worked through his flips and tricks. When he tried one of his more difficult combinations, his fingers failed to grasp the bar at the last moment. He fell to the safety net Leon had secured minutes before, but Snow's heart still dropped. That net wouldn't be there during showtime.

"Sunny says falling during practice prevents it during performance," Byron commented.

Snow released a breath, embarrassed that her fear had been so visible. "His performances are amazing," she admitted. "How long has he been doing this?"

"Hard to know for sure." Byron pushed his hat back far enough to scratch his hairline. "Not even he knows. He saw a circus when he was six or seven, he thinks, and he's been swinging from things ever since. The kid's heart belongs in the air, that's for sure." Byron shivered, his half frown a clear representation of how he felt about "the air."

Byron turned back to his box of props, and Snow watched

Sunny restart from where he'd left off. He swung his legs to gain momentum before transitioning into the same trick that landed him in the net before. She held her breath as he let go of the bar to do his flip, and it felt like an eternity before his fingers reached for the bar again. This time they wrapped around the metal with a secure grip. Her breath came out in a whoosh as she clapped along with other performers on the ground.

"I wonder what it feels like up there."

Snow didn't realize she'd spoken the thought aloud until Byron responded, "I'm sure Sunny would be happy to show you."

"Show me trapeze?" Her stomach looped at the thought. "I could never do that."

"What if it's your act?" Byron tilted his head, running a coin across his knuckles, flipping it between his fingers.

Her heart sank watching him perform the trick as if it didn't even take thought. Based on the more impressive magic acts she'd seen him perform before audiences, the coin trick was probably nothing for him. Like the grace of Sunny's act, the ease of Byron's magic belied years of dedication. They both had years to perfect what they did before audiences. Years of experience Snow could never catch up to or compete with.

Snow shook her head, hugging herself as her gaze returned to Sunny in the air. "I don't have an act. I could never learn something as amazing as what you all do."

"No one here learned their skill overnight."

A clink drew her attention back to Byron in time to see him catch the coin before it could fall to the grass, having bounced off the bench. Red splotches filled his cheeks as he gave her a sheepish grin.

"You'll find your act," he commented, breaking their eye contact by bouncing his gaze away. "I never thought being a clown would become my life passion."

"What did you do before the circus?"

"I volleyed between jobs. I was a grocer for a time. Then I delivered furniture with Gerard." He motioned to the strongman bench pressing an actual bench in one corner of the tent. "I was just getting by, passing the time. It was never my plan to be a performer. If someone told me that I'd become one, I would have said they belonged in an institution. Now I can't imagine my future without this place."

Even if Byron's gaze remained elsewhere while he talked to her, she could see the joy and pride in his eyes as he watched his fellow troupe members prepare their routines. After he fell silent, she turned her attention back to Sunny flipping and twirling through the air. A performer? She'd never dreamed of being one either, but the longer she watched the trapeze, the more her curiosity grew. What did it feel like to fly? To feel nothing but air, even for a few seconds. Would it feel like freedom?

"Do you believe in God, Miss Snow?" Byron broke into her thoughts as he rummaged in his suitcase again.

She stilled, the magic of the moment shattered like glass. Her gaze dropped to the ground, and she scuffed the toe of her brown shoe in the dirt. "I grew up in church."

"Well, I believe in something I call divine appointment, and I can't seem to shake the feeling that your arrival was just that."

She frowned as her stomach curdled. "I doubt there's anything divine about my running away to the circus."

"I wouldn't be so sure. I can't shake the feeling that you're here for a reason." Byron stopped messing with his suitcase to rub his palms on his thighs, one knee bouncing. "Being a helping hand is a worthy purpose, but I wonder if you're here for something more."

I'm here because it was the only thing left that I could do. But the words stuck in her throat. Once upon a time, Snow might have bought into every word he said. She'd bought into it when her beloved guardian promised her that a loving God would never leave her in the wake of her parents' death. But then Chester Combs had left her too. Left her alone with nothing but heartbroken pleas from the depths of her soul to a God who never answered.

In the wake of her silence, Byron licked his lips, his gaze bouncing around the tent again. "All I know is that I wouldn't be here if Gerard hadn't dared me to dream beyond what I thought of myself, and God used it to bring me the biggest blessing of my life. If you let yourself dream, what would you choose to do?"

She twisted the fabric flower in her fingers.

Byron packed his props back into his suitcase and stood to leave. "Just think about it."

She held the flower out. "Don't forget this."

He shook his head, lifting the case by its worn handle. "Keep it."

As he walked away, she stared into the center of the fabric flower, twirling it between her fingers. What would it be like to dare to dream? Daring to leave everything she knew to hop a circus train was the first time she'd dared to do anything, but it was desperation, not imagination, that drove her from her lifelong home in the dead of night. Desperation fueled by the knowledge that if she stayed, it would practically be a death sentence with no escape.

But already this circus was proving to be a more beautiful opportunity than she had ever imagined it to be. Was that by coincidence?

Snow lifted her gaze as Sunny released his hold on the trapeze bar for his final flip through the air. Her heart seemed to leap in her chest with him, leaving behind a stirring like she'd never felt before.

❧

JULY 1910

Catherine fought a wave of fatigue as she shuffled down the hall to what had once been her father's study. She tapped her knuckles on the dark oak door.

"Come in," Ethel's impatient voice drifted under the door.

Catherine slipped into the room. The familiar smell of leather, paper, and ink greeted her, beckoning her to stay among the towering shelves, but the warm feelings soured at the sight of Ethel behind her father's desk.

Ethel shot Catherine a hard look over her spectacles. "What do you need?"

Catherine licked her lips. "I'm feeling good today. I was hoping I could have my father's journal back so I can study how he ran the estate. My twenty-first birthday is fast approaching, and I know I'm not prepared to take everything over."

Ethel sighed as she removed her spectacles. "Yes, you are far from prepared, but I'm afraid there's nothing you can do about that. This illness of yours has rendered you incapable—"

"I'm not—"

"How do you expect to run everything when you barely have the energy to get out of bed once a week?"

"This is my second—"

"When you first fell ill, I know we were hoping for a swift recovery, but I think it's time to consider what happens if you never recover." Ethel stood and paced to the single window in the room. She left no room for Catherine to respond as she continued, "What if you never regain strength? I've tried to avoid the topic for your sake, but if you think you're ready to take responsibility for your parents' estate, you're ready to come to terms with this possibility. You're growing weaker with time, Catherine, not stronger."

Ethel delivered the words unflinching, her tone ringing cold in the quiet room. Tears stung at Catherine's eyes, and she clenched her fists to hold back her growing anger. "I'm going to get better."

"Did you eat your breakfast this morning?"

"Part of it."

Ethel whirled to face Catherine, a condescending frown on her lips. "You won't get better if you don't even eat."

Catherine cringed at the chiding tone, the same one Ethel had used when she was a child misbehaving. She straightened her spine and lifted her chin. "Ethel, I want my father's journal. My parents meant for me to take over the estate and the mines when I come of age, and I have every intention of doing that."

Ethel stared at her for a long moment, and even though Catherine couldn't decipher the look in her eyes, a chill fell down her spine. Without a word, Ethel strode back to the desk and opened one of the drawers. She pulled out the journal and held it up. Willing her legs not to give out, Catherine crossed the room to take the book, but when she grabbed it, Ethel held on.

"I'm trying to help you, Catherine, but I can't if you don't listen to me."

Catherine tugged the book out of her guardian's hand and hugged it to her chest. "I'm thankful for everything you've done since my parents and Chester passed away, but I'm old enough for you to trust my judgment too."

Ethel said nothing as Catherine made her way back to the door.

"Let me know if you have questions about anything you read," Ethel commented as Catherine opened the door. "I've run everything since my husband passed."

"His name was Chester," Catherine whispered.

"What?" Ethel frowned.

"You never say his name. I believe that talking about the

ones we've loved and lost keeps their memories alive in our hearts. Why do you never use his name?"

"What difference does it make what I call him?" The snap in her tone cracked her cold exterior, and anger simmered in her eyes. "He was my husband, and I'll refer to him as such."

Catherine bit the inside of her cheek, trying to find words to express the emotions swirling inside of her. How could someone go over six years without speaking the name of their beloved? Did his memory pain Ethel that much? She never seemed like a heartbroken widow. Not in the way Catherine felt like a heartbroken orphan after the loss of her parents. Ethel and Chester never showed affection in the way her parents had, but they must have cared for each other at some point to marry.

Ethel returned to her work, and seeing that she had determined the conversation over, Catherine slipped from the room without saying anything further. With her father's journal back in her hands, she let out a deep breath.

Walking to her room on her own two legs, Catherine could almost believe her claim that she would get better, but no matter how hard she tried, she could not ignore the decaying feeling in her core. The aches in her joints were a reminder of how her own mortality refused to be silenced.

Catherine paused in the hall, her hand supporting her against the wall as the fatigue caught up to her yet again. For a fleeting moment, she wondered if trying so hard for a future was worth it. She'd tried to tell herself to carry on for her parents, but could she even make them proud if they'd passed on to paradise? Surely someone in paradise cared little for earthly matters.

That meant Chester wouldn't see how she fought so hard to survive and push on despite all of the setbacks thrown into her path too. He was the one who, once upon a time, had instilled in her the determination to never give up.

If they could see her, she knew they would all be proud.

Catherine lifted her chin as she stepped into the quiet solace of her room. Even if it was only for that day, she would dare to dream. She would dare to dream of her future ahead and the possibility of taking up her parents' mantle. Maybe if she dreamed hard enough, the bleakness of the time ahead of her would brighten.

CHAPTER 4

NOVEMBER 1904

Snow grunted in frustration as her fingers brushed the bar but failed to catch hold. She bounced into the net, the ropes scraping her bare arms. After the bouncing of the net stilled, she lay on her back, glaring at the cursed bar above. Why couldn't she figure out the transition?

Sunny finished his transition, ending by mounting the rise—all terms Snow had managed to learn under Sunny's tutelage. After completing his agile, catlike moves, he peered over the edge of the platform at Snow.

"Are you all right?" he called down to her.

"I'm fine." She dragged herself upright and clawed her way to the edge of the net.

Sunny watched her with uncertainty in his eyes, his dark brows drawn in worry. "Perhaps you should take a break."

She nodded before descending the ladder to the ground. Stalking over to the stands, Snow refused to look up as Sunny continued his routine. How could she expect to become a trapeze artist if she couldn't even leap from one bar to the other?

She sat on the lowest row of seats, but the frustration

burning in her chest refused to let her sit still. Circling around to the side of the stands where the performers practicing in the ring couldn't see her, Snow began running through stretches and drills Sunny taught her to improve her mobility and flexibility.

Snow focused on stretching every muscle she could, repeating backflips and reaches until her muscles responded how she desired. The burning in her limbs was a minor distraction she was determined to get past.

The tights and fitted silk bodysuit she wore allowed her body to move however she told it to, and after several months practicing in it, she'd learned not to be embarrassed by the tightness of the fabric. Everyone in the circus was used to the unconventional attire required to perform the acts.

"Titus, you're up!" Ambrose bellowed from the main ring.

Snow paused with her arms stretched above her head in preparation for another flip when Titus emerged from under the stands. He gave her a groggy smile before walking away. Grass clung to the back of his pants and shirt, and as he sauntered across the big top, he rolled his neck and shook out his arms.

Before Titus could swing onto the bare back of the large black mare, Ambrose brushed off his backside. Once on the magnificent beast, Titus shot his brother the same groggy, lopsided grin.

Ambrose led the mare into the ring, and while he worked her up to a canter, Titus continued to stretch his arms from his seat on her bare back. Once the mare reached a full canter, he pushed himself into a standing position. Even though she had seen the routine dozens of times, Snow found herself captured by the anticipation of what came next.

To her surprise, instead of flipping or twirling into his first trick, Titus nodded to Ambrose. When Ambrose returned the nod, Titus bent over the mare's neck and removed the lead from her bridle. The mare continued in her wide circles, and Titus flipped into a handstand to begin his act.

Snow held her breath, waiting for the mare to lose focus or for something to go wrong with this new stunt, but Titus continued through his routine as smoothly as ever. Somehow he kept the mare circling the ring without Ambrose's help.

"All it takes is knowing there's at least one pair of eyes on him, and Titus becomes a complete ham."

Snow jumped in surprise when Ambrose's voice came from beside her. Completely mesmerized, she had failed to notice him exit the ring.

"What if the mare gets out of hand?" Snow asked. "You aren't there to help him."

"Titus knows what he's doing." Ambrose shrugged his shoulders as he crossed his arms, feet planted a shoulder-width apart. The looped lead hung loose from one hand.

Snow tracked Titus around the ring, her heart sinking the longer she watched his flawless practice. Above his head Sunny flipped across the trapeze.

"I don't think I could ever be like Sunny or Titus," she confessed. "I think I'm trying to learn too late."

"You don't have years of experience under your belt, but that doesn't mean you started too late. That just means you have a lot of practice ahead of you," Ambrose stated with a matter-of-fact tone as he kept his eyes on his brother.

Snow bit her lip. How many times had Sunny or Leon or any of the others said something to her of that effect in the six months she'd been trying to learn the trapeze?

Practice makes progress.

You'll never get better if you don't practice.

But even after learning and practicing for six months, even after trying over and over again until her palms bled, Snow couldn't seem to find the same dazzling abilities in herself that she saw in the others. How much time did it take?

"Titus makes it look so easy," Snow muttered. "I don't think I've ever seen him fall."

"Titus's one fatal flaw is that he hates people seeing his flaws." Ambrose paused to take a handkerchief from his pocket and swipe it under his nose. "Even when it's only the performers around, he hates his imperfections being on display. What everyone witnesses during public practice is his perfect routine, but if you want to see what it takes to get here, come back to the big top at midnight tonight."

"At midnight?" she echoed.

He shrugged as he returned the cloth to his pocket. "You'll be surprised at what you see."

They lapsed into silence, and after a few minutes of watching Titus circle the ring with his immaculate routine, Snow turned to practice her drills again. This time she tried to land a handless backflip, another move that Sunny tried to teach her, but she failed to figure out. Like the times she had practiced before, she couldn't find the right arc of her body, and instead of landing on her feet, she landed in a heap on the grass after failing to catch herself with her arms.

Embarrassment heated her face when Ambrose held out his hand to help her up.

"I don't understand what I'm doing wrong," she huffed as she staggered to her feet, her shoulder aching from the awkward landing.

"It's your posture before you take off. Pay closer attention to how you're holding your back."

Ambrose held up his hand in a silent command for her to wait, and then he took two wide steps to the side. After checking behind him, he swung his arms and bent his knees. In one fluid motion he sprang into the air, his legs flying over his head. He landed squarely on his feet with his knees still bent.

Snow's eyes widened. "You're an acrobat!"

He lifted his palms in a shrug, a smile tugging one side of his mouth.

"Why don't you perform?"

Ambrose shook his head as he wiped his nose with the handkerchief again. "Titus is the performer. There was a time we had a routine together, but he has always been better."

Snow chewed on her lip as she considered her next question. She didn't want to hurt his feelings. "Does it... Does it bother you to be in the background while he receives all the recognition for his talent? I've seen the way you are with the horses. You have a talent of your own, but nobody notices when he's twirling around you. And now he's developing an act where he doesn't even need you."

"I love the horses, but Titus lives for the thrill of the performance. Performing was work for me." He walked over to the stands to sit, and he waited for Snow to join him before he continued. "I think Leon saw that when we first started forming the circus, and he was the one who gave me permission to step back from performing. I thought maybe I was a failure for it, but in time, I found that I got my thrill from caring for the animals. Now that we're growing, my expertise with animals is becoming more and more in demand. So to up his performances, Titus decided to learn how to control the horses himself, and that frees me to work on animal care behind the scenes. I'm excited for this new opportunity for both of us."

"Maybe I was meant to stay behind the scenes too." Snow drew her knees up to her chest and hugged them.

Ambrose raised his eyebrows. "Titus comes alive with the cheers of the crowd. I find my thrill every time Leon tells me we'll be adding a new animal to our herd. It's like a challenge to learn how they communicate and to learn their individual needs and personalities. I live for it the same way Titus lives for the adrenaline. Are you going to tell me you get a thrill from mending costumes or selling peanuts?"

She chewed on her lip instead of responding.

"When you're really passionate about something, you don't just give one or two tries and give up. The bond I have with animals doesn't happen instantaneously." Ambrose gestured at Titus's handstand on horseback. "He practices for hours to become like that, and I work for hours with the animals. We love the job, but we respect our passions enough to devote the time to master them."

Snow's heart wanted to rouse at his passionate words. To march across the big top to the trapeze and try again until she got it, but the aches in her body kept her rooted in place. What if this wasn't something she was physically capable of? What if time and passion wasn't enough to learn the complicated maneuvers?

Snow raised her gaze to Sunny on the trapeze, and she fought against the hopelessness that tried to consume her thoughts. No matter how much she tried to accept maybe this wasn't meant for her, one look up there set off the burning desire in her chest to figure out what it felt like to fly.

With his hands braced on his knees, Ambrose pushed himself to his feet. "I know we all strive to perfect our acts, but perfection is an illusion that disappeared with the garden of Eden. Each of us has an obstacle we must overcome every day we answer the call God placed on us." He shook his handkerchief between his fingers. "Obstacles like allergies to the horses or the hay or both."

She raised her eyebrows. "That's why you're always sneezing and sniffling. Yet you still work with the animals."

He shrugged with a lopsided grin that resembled his brother. "What can I say? Can't live with them, but I know I couldn't live without them either. When you truly believe in what you're doing, you can find a way past the shortcomings. You think Titus is flawless, but I'm telling you, come back here at midnight. You might find a new perspective."

The tent erupted in applause as Titus dropped to sit on the mare's back, using his heels against her side to slow her canter to a walk. Ambrose saluted Snow with two fingers before he jogged across the grass to meet his brother at the edge of the ring. He greeted the mare with a rub to her velvety nose and allowed her to nibble a sugar cube from his palm. She gave him an affectionate nuzzle to the neck in return, which made Ambrose grin and sneeze simultaneously.

SNOW SLID OFF HER COT, GROPING IN THE DARKNESS OF THE TENT for her trousers and shirt. When she had decided to pursue the trapeze, Sunny gifted her a few of his clothes for her to tailor to her own body. The boys' clothes were easier to work and practice in, and it saved the dresses Leon bought for when she needed to look respectable in front of audiences as she helped sell peanuts.

She pulled the clothes on over her nightgown before slipping from the tent. The crisp November air kissed her cheeks, and Snow brushed her hair from her eyes as she wove through the dark, quiet tents that made up the circus camp. The light of the moon guided her toward the big top.

The tent flaps hung closed, but when Snow parted one canvas enough to peek inside, a single gas lamp reflected into a series of mirrors to light the center ring.

Even though Ambrose said he would be here, somehow she was still surprised to see Titus guiding two horses around the ring. He stood on their backs, one foot on each, and used the reins to adjust their strides until they fell into step.

Once they cantered in rhythm, Titus stepped onto the black mare and urged the brown one to move over a couple of feet to create a gap between the two. He stood steady on the black mare for a moment, letting the two horses make another circle.

Then, with a deep breath, he sprang off the black mare into a flip. His feet angled to land on the brown mare's back, but his timing failed. He slid off her rump, landing in a heap in the dirt.

With a gasp, Snow started to pull the tent flap open to rush to his aid, but he dragged himself upright. As he brushed the dirt off his clothes, his whistle slowed the horses to a stop. The brown mare danced in place nervously as he approached. He took a moment to stroke her nose and whisper to her before he dared to remount.

Snow drew the tent flap closed to conceal herself as he repeated the same routine until he reached the point of the flip. Once again, he missed his mark and fell, but this time he fell on the mare's back and grabbed her mane to keep from crashing to the dirt.

Snow remained enraptured as Titus continued the same routine in an endless loop. Each fall and bobble caused him to start again, and start again he did. With each circle around the ring, he landed closer to his mark, made a cleaner arc, or landed less awkwardly than before.

Then came the final arc that ended with his feet planted firmly on the center of the brown horse's back. Titus dropped to sit, pumping his fist in the air. He let out a whoop and patted the mare's neck. Snow clasped her hands over her mouth to resist the urge to cheer and clap along.

She grinned from the shadows, watching the pure triumph light his face. Determination settled in her chest like a rock as she stepped back from the tent, letting the flap fall closed. She stretched her arms and back before straightening into her opening position. Trying to remember the nuances of Sunny's instructions, as well as Ambrose's demonstration, Snow launched herself into a handless backflip. Like every time she had tried it before, she landed ungracefully in the grass, but she pushed herself to her feet again.

Channeling the same tireless energy as Titus, she repeated

the steps over and over, trying each time to pay attention to what threw her off. She gritted her teeth in determination as she repeatedly leapt feet over head. Her fingers and toes grew chilled in the cold November air even as sweat gathered under her shirt.

"Pay closer attention to how you're holding your back." Ambrose's voice echoed in her mind as Snow commanded every muscle to bend her body to her will. Her body flipped, feet above her head, and her feet landed in the grass. She froze, her knees still bent with the impact of her landing. A smile slowly spread across her face before she sprang upright, pumping her fist in the air.

A new determination ignited in her chest like a burning coal. Tomorrow she would practice the bar transition again, no matter how many times it took.

~

AUGUST 1910

"Ethel?" Catherine peered into her father's study.

Ethel looked up from where she was gathering papers off the desk and stuffing them into a satchel. "What is it?" Impatience seeped into her tone.

Catherine stepped into the room, hugging her father's journal to her chest. "Would you be able to help me decipher these accounts? I want to understand how my father's accounting system worked."

"I don't have time." Ethel resumed her packing.

"You told me to ask if I had any questions, and I do. There are two months left until—"

"I told you, I don't have time." Ethel slammed one of the desk drawers shut. "I'm already late for a meeting at the mines, and the rest of my day is swamped with appointments."

"The mines?" Catherine straightened her back. "I'd like to go. I haven't been there since Chester passed—"

"No." Ethel's harsh response echoed through the large room as she donned a forest-green jacket with puffy sleeves over her cream blouse. "What if we travel all the way to the mines and you become fatigued or sick? Bringing you all the way back home will ruin my schedule."

Catherine gripped the journal cover, trying not to let her mounting frustration show. Her gaze drifted to the window. "Then I suppose I'll take a ride through the orchard."

Ethel released a pent-up sigh as she advanced to the door. "Really, Catherine? You need to save your strength. Pushing yourself when you think you're finally recovering will worsen your health again. I heard you practicing the piano the other day. It sounds like your scales could use more work. That might be a better use of your time."

Catherine stepped away from the door without a word as her guardian breezed out. The silence of the empty office seemed to cave in on her, pressing on her already-downtrodden soul. She stumbled a few steps further into the room before collapsing into an overstuffed leather chair. The little bit of courage she'd mustered to request help from her guardian fled the room as quickly as Ethel had.

Catherine sat unmoving for several minutes, having no desire or energy to return to her room. The comforting smell of aged leather surrounded her as she slumped in the seat. Her father's journal laid in her lap, her fingertips running over the smooth cover. Something stirred in her memory as she sat there. Like a memory relived in a dream, a broken, distorted image filled her mind of her father sitting in this chair, a book open on his lap.

She closed her eyes and leaned her head back as she focused on the memory, trying to bring it clearer into view. She took a deep breath to draw in the smell of the leather and the books around her, but the light undertone of Ethel's perfume suffocated the memories. She took shallower breaths to focus.

The longer she dwelled on the image of her father in the chair, the more the scene seemed to come together in her mind. Catherine could feel her younger self on hesitant tiptoes, making her way to where he sat. Instead of being brushed off for interrupting, his strong arms drew her onto his lap. With arms stretched on either side of her, he reopened his book to show her what he was studying. Even if she didn't understand a word of the book, she was happy to settle back against his chest and let his deep voice reverberate over her.

Tears flooded Catherine's eyes at the hazy memory. How long had it been since she remembered anything from her youth? It seemed that whatever was stealing her strength was stealing her memories too.

She opened her eyes to gaze around the room. Her gaze skittered over the floor-to-ceiling bookcases and landed on the fireplace. A large mirror framed in gold covered the expanse of the green wall above the fireplace. Catherine pushed herself to her feet and made her way to it.

A memory stirred in her mind. A portrait. A portrait of the three Penners, but no matter how hard she tried to remember, she couldn't make the faces form into clear images. How long had the portrait been missing? Why was it missing?

"It's good to remember, Catherine, even if remembering hurts."

Catherine held her breath, the gentle whisper ringing in her ears as if spoken by a ghost over her shoulder.

"Remembering in pain is better than forgetting. What's forgotten can't be returned."

She rested her hands on the mantle, staring at her gaunt image in the vast mirror. She willed herself to remember. To return to her mind what was forgotten. Even though the faces of the portrait refused to materialize, other images came together like partial photographs. Her mother's smile as she guided Catherine through her studies. Her father's broad back as Catherine rode behind him on horseback through the orchard. Her guardian holding her in front of the portrait, encouraging her to turn her face from his neck to gaze on her parents' faces. It was Chester's voice that encouraged her to remember and never forget while her parents' deaths were a fresh wound in her tender, young heart.

Catherine gripped the mantle, the edge of the wood biting into her soft fingertips. How many memories had she forgotten? When she looked at the stolen space, the memories seemed to fall away, wiped from her mind by a strong hand and stern presence.

The guardian she loved and thrived under was replaced by his rigid wife, a woman determined to keep Catherine in her place. Under an embroidery hoop. At the keys of a piano. Far from the safe haven of her father's office. Catherine's gaze met her own in the mirror, but a wisp of a woman stared back at her with sunken, dark-rimmed eyes and hollow cheeks. Her skin was so pale she could have been an apparition.

Catherine turned away from the mantle as images of Ethel filled her mind and crowded out the beautiful memories of her parents and Chester. Chasing away the darkening thoughts, Catherine fled the office, willing her knees to hold her up. She made her way into the hall, and instead of going to the piano room as Ethel had suggested, she continued to her bedroom.

She paced over to the window where she could have a clear view of the apple orchard that made up part of her family's estate. The pride and joy and hard work of generations of Penners. The dark green leaves danced on the breeze as if teasing and beckoning her to come out to them.

A restless stirring seeped into Catherine's spirit. The aches of her body told her Ethel was right. Her days were numbered and her efforts limited, but the restless stirring grew stronger with those thoughts.

She had already accomplished what even Chester had deemed impossible. She returned what was once forgotten, even if in snippets. She would prove herself to Ethel too. She would find strength again. She would learn the ropes of her father's estate to take over where he left off. If for no other reason, she would do it to taste freedom one more time.

A knock on the door broke through her thoughts. "Come in," Catherine called without turning from the window.

"Mrs. Combs thought some tea would be good for you," the maid, Ruth, said as she shuffled into the room.

Catherine turned to watch her carry the tray to the table by the chair. A plate of Danishes sat next to the pot of tea on the tray.

"These are apple Danishes made with some of the first fruit plucked off the limb this morning," Ruth declared proudly. "Mrs. Combs said you were feeling good today, and she thought teatime might give you the energy you need to get through the rest of the day."

Catherine wordlessly walked over to the tea set, and a brief thought flashed through her mind that she tried to squash: Did Ethel truly care? More than likely, she'd sent Ruth with tea to make sure Catherine didn't try to sneak out for a ride.

That thought made her want to reject the tea, but doing so was pointless. It would prove nothing to Ethel. Catherine sank into her chair and motioned for Ruth to pour the tea.

After filling the delicate cup, Ruth respectfully took a step back. "Is there anything else I can do for you?"

"No, thank you." Catherine gave her a soft smile as she picked up one of the flaky Danishes.

Ruth slipped from the room, and Catherine turned her attention to the window. She watched a bird sail through the air as she bit into the warm pastry, and her heart yearned to join that bird. Soaring and free.

CHAPTER 5

OCTOBER 1905

Snow giggled in anticipation as Sunny held his hands over her eyes.

"This feels ridiculous," she muttered and elbowed him lightly in the ribs.

"It's all part of the big reveal," Sunny teased. "Are you ready for the surprise?"

"Show me already!" She laughed and tugged at his arms.

"Three... two... one!" Sunny yanked his hands away. "Tada!"

Snow blinked as she stared at the side of the train car. Stretching almost the height of the car was a full-color poster. Two illustrated acrobats filled the center, their knees hooked over separate bars but their hands reached toward each other, their fingertips a breath apart. Snow sucked in a breath as she stepped closer to take in the detail. The dark-haired female wore a glittering leotard, and the male was clad in a matching tight-fitted shirt and pants. He grinned at the female, his eyes nearly disappearing with his smile.

"Gravity Defying Duo" stretched above the couple in a bold, flourishing font, and the bottom dared onlookers to "come see the world's highest dance, thirty feet above the earth."

Snow turned on her heels to face Leon and Sunny, who watched with matching grins. "Is this... is this real?"

Leon nodded as he stepped forward. "The advertisements for your debut performance the day after tomorrow are being distributed as we speak."

"The day after—?" She gasped, her mouth falling open again.

Sunny laughed at her shocked expression.

Leon shook his head with a chuckle. "I thought for sixteen we should come up with something better than a last-minute cake like last year."

Snow turned back to the poster to soak in its beauty. Her heart hammered against her sternum, and she struggled to draw in a complete breath. She wanted to focus on the fact they remembered her birthday and planned the most amazing surprise, but instead, fear ate at her belly as she stared at the illustrated version of herself.

She started chewing on the edge of her bottom lip. Was she ready?

Leon rested a hand on her shoulder, pulling her from her racing thoughts. "I know this might be quite the shock for you, but I've been watching the routine you and Sunny have developed." He squeezed her shoulder. "You're ready."

Snow could find no words to reply, but before she had to, the clear sound of a bell rang across the circus camp.

"We better get some grub while there's still some left," Sunny said.

Shoving her fears out of her mind, Snow followed after Sunny. She walked through the familiar routine of standing in line at the chuck wagon to receive her tin plate of food. Beans. A bit of brisket. A dry roll. The food was a far cry from the cuisine she'd once enjoyed, prepared by a quality chef, but after a long day of hard training, she had learned that the flavor wasn't as important as nutrients.

The golden glow of sunset fell on the circus family as they

spread out to find seats on hay bales arranged in rings around the clearing. Snow followed in Sunny's footsteps to join the other six brothers in their circle. Ambrose stoked the beginning of a fire to ward off the evening chill, and other circles around the clearing followed suit in lighting their own fires. There would be no performance that night, only relaxing and reveling in the day.

Snow sank onto a hay bale by herself, her mind still wrapped up in that poster. The seven brothers' jolly conversation buzzed around her as she stared into the fire and picked at her plate.

She replayed every part of her routine with Sunny in her memory, highlighting every area she had fumbled in their last practice. What if she failed her performance and Leon realized he made a mistake in giving her a chance? It didn't matter that Sunny had been training her for over a year. She still made mistakes right and left.

After Sunny took her almost-empty plate back to the chuck wagon, she remained rooted in place. The light of the fire danced with the shadows of the night around her. Snow drew her legs up on the bale and hugged her knees to her chest. Ambrose cracked some joke that sent the others roaring with laughter, Gerard's laugh booming the loudest, but Snow didn't even pretend to have heard or join in the laughter. The weight of her thoughts kept her trapped in her mind.

Titus booted Ambrose off his hay bale so he could stretch out, settling his flat cap over his face. Maximilien lit his after-dinner cigar, and Leon excused himself to finish work in the circus office wagon. Ambrose wasted no time in taking over Leon's hay bale, still stoking the fire with a long stick.

Usually, Snow relished the nights when they had nothing to do but relax around the fire. As much as she enjoyed watching the circus performances and selling popcorn or peanuts, she savored these quiet moments when she could be part of a family again. Even if she said nothing, the warmth of their interactions with each other reached her heart. It resurfaced memories of happiness last felt in the loving arms of her parents.

But tonight a shadow loomed over Snow's happiness, and it was more than the shadow of the big top that the moon cast over them.

How many times had she seen her happiness end?

No matter how hard she tried to ignore the thoughts, with each passing day it grew harder to ignore the fear. Even if they had welcomed Snow with open arms from the moment she stumbled onto their train, the brothers still didn't know the whole truth about who she was or what she ran from in her past. If they knew, it could ruin her position at the circus.

But now, if her debut performance failed to live up to their expectations, Snow wouldn't have to wait for the truth of her past to come out for everything to be ruined. The thought left her stomach twisting in a way that threatened to heave her dinner.

One by one the brothers bid the circle goodnight until Snow and Sunny were alone beside the dying embers of the fire. Sunny scooted onto the same hay bale as Snow, and he poked at the fire with the stick Ambrose had abandoned. She leaned her head on his muscular shoulder, trying to draw some peace or strength from his presence. On the trapeze, whenever her stomach twisted from the heights, it was his strong presence that stabilized her.

"Are you ready for bed?" Sunny asked as he dropped the stick, giving up on rekindling the embers.

She blew out a breath without lifting her head. "I don't know if I'll ever sleep between now and our performance."

Sunny rested his hand on her knee. "I know what it feels like to be nervous for your first performance. I'll never forget mine."

"What if I'm not ready?" She squeezed her eyes shut as she voiced the question that had been eating her alive from the moment she saw the poster. Alone, Sunny was a spectacle worth beholding, drawing crowds from miles around, but what if her amateur performance brought him down? He worked too hard to deserve that.

The illustrated image of herself flashed through her memory. That girl looked elegant, graceful, beautiful. She still felt like an awkward stowaway, seconds away from messing everything up. How could they be the same person?

Snow was so wrapped in her whirling thoughts that she didn't realize Sunny never responded to her voiced fear. She raised her head to search his expression in the moonlight.

"I don't want to fail and bring you embarrassment," she whispered.

Instead of replying, Sunny stood. He grabbed her hand at the same time to pull her up. "I want to show you another surprise."

"Another one?" she squeaked as he pulled her into the heart of the camp. She didn't know if she could take another big surprise.

"Leon wanted to save this one for your actual birthday," Sunny explained, not loosening his grip on her hand. Snow focused on the calloused palm that felt the same as the day it pulled her aboard the train. Most days in practice, it was the only thing that kept her from falling to the net below.

A net that wouldn't be there in the performance.

She shuddered and held his hand tighter.

Sunny paused at the costumer's trailer to ease open the door. "Leon should have known that if he wanted to keep a secret that long, he had no business telling me."

Once inside the trailer together, Sunny drew the door shut and groped in the darkness until he found a lantern to light. Then he turned to position Snow in front of the full-length mirror.

"Wait here. With your eyes closed." He put his hand over her eyes.

Snow obediently closed them, even though it made her

stomach start twisting all over again. She chewed on her lip as Sunny rummaged somewhere behind her, and a moment later he draped something in front of her, holding it against her shoulders.

"Okay, open," he said from where he stood behind her.

She opened her eyes to see the sparkling red leotard Sunny held up to her frame. He grinned over her shoulder.

"What do you think?" he asked.

She looked down at the beautiful piece, running her hand down the length of glittering gems. In the shadowy light of the single lamp, Snow could picture how the silk leotard would glitter and display under the big top lights. It might have been the most beautiful costume she had ever laid eyes on.

Sunny nudged her from behind. "Look at yourself in the mirror."

Snow obediently raised her eyes to the mirror again, taking in the costume over her own trousers and shirt.

"That looks like a graceful performer to me, ready for the center ring," Sunny declared.

Snow pinched the sides of the costume and held it to her waist to see how the piece might look on her. She focused on hers and Sunny's reflections in the slender mirror. Both had grown over the last year and a half, and he had even managed to catch up to her in height so that they looked eye to eye. Even though his strength would always surpass hers, her limbs had filled out with muscle she hadn't known possible before. Her creamy skin still paled in comparison to his impressive tan, but there was a color to her cheeks that she could almost consider a sun-kissed glow.

And maybe it wasn't only her physique that had grown in that time. For all the fear she carried about the performance, Snow knew she possessed a confidence that she didn't have before. A confidence that allowed her to hold her spine straight and carry her head high. There was a new grace that flowed through her movements. All thanks to the love and care of the seven brothers around her.

Staring at her reflection with Sunny behind her, Snow could almost believe his words about the graceful performer he saw.

"You belong here, Snow." Sunny's breath tickled the hair along her neck. "No matter what heartache brought you here, God brought you to us for a reason."

That fleeting confidence dissipated. "I wasn't brought by God. I ran away," she blurted, unable to contain the burning secret she knew would surface eventually.

Sunny let the leotard drop and stepped around her to search her face with his gaze. "Snow—"

"You deserve to know the full truth." She hugged her arms around herself, turning her face away. "I told you that I was an orphan with nothing left, but some people probably wouldn't view it that way. My full name is Catherine P—"

"Penner," Sunny finished for her.

She stilled before slowly meeting his gaze again. "You know?"

"Catherine Penner, only daughter of Harry and Eugenia Penner. Sole heiress to the Penner Coal Mines and estate." He spoke the words with a matter-of-fact tone as if reading it off a paper. Then he shrugged.

She stared at him in disbelief. "Did you know this whole time? Does everyone else know too?"

"Not the *whole* time, but it didn't take me long to figure out. As far as I'm aware, no one else knows."

Snow sank onto a nearby trunk. "All this time, you kept my secret."

"People need to give me a little more credit. I'm not the worst secret keeper out there." Sunny sat on the trunk across from her. "I figured there was a reason you kept it hidden, and it wasn't my place to ruin that."

"How did you know?"

A pensive expression passed over his face as his gaze fell to the floor. "I admit that cutting your hair threw me off for a bit, but I couldn't shake that I knew you from somewhere. Some newspaper clippings and a little research led me to my answer. Anyone familiar with your family would probably figure it out eventually."

"What if someone else knows already?" She buried her face in her hands with a groan. Was this a good sign? If everyone knew the truth and never said anything, maybe they never planned to. Maybe no one would feel responsible to send her back to where she belonged. Maybe... they didn't care about her past life.

"I don't think anyone else knows."

"But my family is recognizable enough that you found out," she countered.

"Because I worked at your mines."

Snow sat back at his forceful declaration. She blinked, trying to understand. "You worked... When?"

Sunny closed his eyes as he rubbed his brow. "I think it was close to six years ago now. It was before Leon found me and we formed this circus. I, too, was a desperate runaway, and I tried to make a living in the mining industry at first. Small but strong boys were valuable. I remember you because you visited the mines once when I worked there."

Snow searched her memory. She loved visiting the mines with her father and then later on with Chester, and she saw the young, dirty faces that made up the workforce. She knew they weren't any older than herself, but sitting across from Sunny now, the reality of it took on a different light. Guilt played through her chest as she tried to remember a particular young Asian boy, but try as she might, she could find no memory of him. To her, he must have been one of the many workers.

"Sunny, I'm sorry—"

He held up a hand. "It was a short part of my history. The

point is that you aren't the only runaway who found a home in this circus, but unlike you, I didn't leave a legacy behind. I left a sister."

As he gazed into the lantern flame, Snow thought she saw his glistening eyes redden.

She reached across the gap between them to take his hand. "You have a sister?" She hoped her grip could hold the same anchoring presence that his did for her.

"A sister. And a brother. And somewhere out in this big world, I think I even still have a father." He shook his head, closing his eyes. "But we lived with my aunt and uncle after my mother passed away. As soon as he was old enough, my brother left to make his own way in the world. So when I thought I was old enough, I did the same."

"How old were you?"

"Eleven."

Snow released a slow breath. She tried to picture Sunny as an eleven-year-old, and the image she conjured was a small, spindly youth with the same boyish face she knew. Her heart broke picturing him crawling through mining tunnels, covered in coal dust and dirt.

"My sister begged me not to leave her too, but I had overheard my aunt and uncle talking about what a burden I was. I decided to take care of myself, but I couldn't stand the cramped darkness, so I didn't stay at the mines long. Instead, I realized pretty quickly that my agility made it easy to pick pockets, and moral lines tend to blur when your stomach is empty enough. Who knows where I would have ended up next if I hadn't tried to pick Leon's pocket and failed. Byron would call it a divine appointment."

She bit her lip. "He said the same thing when I first arrived at the circus."

Sunny raised his eyebrows. "I'm inclined to agree. None of

us knew it when you hopped our train, but this troupe needed you, Snow."

"Anyone who found out about my true identity wouldn't agree. They would probably say I belong where I came from. I belong to my guardian, according to the law."

"Do you regret leaving?"

She hesitated. Snow couldn't deny there were times when she wondered what would become of her family's legacy if she wasn't there to carry it on, but then she remembered that five years stood between her legally assuming control of her parents' affairs. Five more years under Ethel's thumb seemed unbearable.

"No," Snow admitted. "I don't. Do you regret running?"

Sunny released a slow breath. "I regret leaving my sister the same way our father and brother left us, but I wouldn't trade this circus family for anything. Leon told me a couple of days ago that Charleston is going to be one of our stops soon, and I hope God will give me a chance to make things right with my sister."

Snow stiffened as blood rushed to her head. "Charleston?"

He nodded. "While we're in town, I want to try to find my sister again and apologize for leaving. I know I can't make everything I did right, but I think if I can at least make sure she's okay, it'll help me put some guilt to rest. The whole point about bringing that up is to show you we all came from something. I left my family. Some of the other guys did too. Some left jobs and careers, but somehow we all ended up here together, where we belong."

Even as Sunny continued his passionate speech, Snow struggled to draw in a full breath as her chest tightened. Charleston. The place she once called home.

"Snow?" Sunny wiggled her arm, still holding onto her hand.

Her lips parted, but she couldn't say anything. Fear paralyzed her.

Sunny moved onto the trunk next to her, using his other hand to cup her cheek. "Snow, are you okay?"

"I'm going to be recognized in Charleston." She stared at him, wide-eyed. "As soon as anyone knows the truth about who I am, I'll be forced to go back."

"Hey, it's going to be all right."

She shook her head, leaning away from his touch. "You don't know that."

"Maybe I don't, but I trust the One who brought you here. And I trust that He's going to work everything out for our good, one way or another."

She ripped her hand out of his and stood from the trunk. "You don't know that," she said with more force than intended.

Sunny sat back on the trunk, his gaze searching her face. "I do."

She turned her back to him, rubbing her temple as she closed her eyes. Unexpected memories bubbled to the surface of her mind. Memories of a beloved guardian with a contagious joy and unwavering faith.

"Catherine, God will never leave you nor forsake you. He promises that."

Tears misted Snow's vision as the image of Chester overwhelmed her. He had been a tall man with blazing red hair and freckled skin that tended to burn in sunlight, but something in Sunny's spirit reminded her of Chester. They both possessed a warmth that made her want to draw close, that made her want to believe in every word they said about God and His faithfulness. It had been her lifeline after the death of her parents.

"I can't believe that," Snow choked out. "Not after God's taken everything else from me already."

How long after Chester died had she cried out to God before resigning herself to believing He didn't hear her? She'd begged Him to send someone, to bring light into her life again. She'd prayed—even if it was an impossible miracle—for God to bring

Chester or her parents back to her. Yet despite her desperate prayers through endless tears, she knew He wasn't listening.

Sunny stood from the trunk and enveloped her in his strong embrace. "You belong here, Snow, and I'm not going to let you go."

Snow buried her face in his shoulder, gripping the back of his shirt in her fingers. "Then promise me you won't tell anyone else the truth about who I am."

"You know they won't care—"

She held on tighter as he started to pull back. "Promise me. I can't ever go back to Ethel, and as long as no one else knows, I don't have to."

He sighed. "I promise."

Snow nodded, relishing the safety of his embrace for a moment longer. If anyone found them in the semidark costume trailer like this, tongues would wag. The story would spread through the circus like wildfire, growing with each new rendition, but she didn't care.

Snow was already aware of how the other brothers teased Sunny on her behalf. They noticed every time their hands touched outside of practice, every smile he sent her way, every minute they spent together, but Sunny never said anything to her about their teasing. So she ignored it. But she couldn't deny how safe she felt in his arms, whether it was when they soared through the air or sat on a trunk in a costume trailer. He knew the full truth about her past, and he never pushed her away.

As they pulled apart, her gaze caught on the leotard he had draped over the mirror. The crystals on the bodice winked at her. Snow didn't know if she could let herself believe in God's promises again, but what if she let herself believe in Sunny's words the same way she'd let herself believe in Chester's? God had always been silent and distant from her pleas, but Sunny was right there. Tangible, within reach, and promising to not let her go.

With him, her future could be bright if she let it. Her debut performance could be the first of many at Sunny's side. A promising career with a wonderful partner.

Sunny cupped her face again, forcing her to meet his eyes. "Will you be all right tonight?"

Snow mustered a genuine smile as she touched the back of his hand. "Thanks to you, I think so."

"We should get to bed if we're going to be worth anything in practice tomorrow." Sunny turned to grab the leotard off the mirror.

Snow helped him return the trailer to the state they'd found it in, and outside the trailer door, Sunny paused to give her one last hug and bid her goodnight.

As she watched him walk away in the moonlight, Snow tried to return her mind to the peace that came with his strong presence. She dwelled on the feeling that his hug had left her with, and her heart kindled with warmth.

Maybe... maybe the other brothers' whispers and teasing was becoming reality. She'd never met a boy that made her want to build those sorts of dreams before, and under Ethel's tutelage, marriage seemed more like a life sentence than a beautiful possibility. But everything she once thought and believed seemed to change the longer she stayed with the circus.

Sunny cast one last smile over his shoulder before slipping into the tent he shared with Ambrose and Titus, and Snow finally turned to walk to her own tent. She looked up at the almost full moon as she walked. For a rare moment, she allowed her heart the pleasure of lingering on the edge of blissful daydreams for the future. It felt dangerous to let her heart and mind run in such a way. The higher the hopes, the harder the fall, after all. But tonight, she couldn't stop herself. She'd finally found something worth hoping in.

∼

SEPTEMBER 1910

Catherine sat in the chair by the window, and by the minute, a familiar ache seeped into her bones. Her strength was disappearing again. She shouldn't be surprised. Every time she dared to hope her health was improving, she would take a turn for the worse.

Catherine turned her gaze to the pen and paper on the table by her chair. For some reason, every time her health would take another dip, she became introspective and couldn't resist the urge to write another letter. No matter how many letters went unanswered, she found herself writing another. And another. Maybe it was some futile way of trying to reconnect with the last time she felt whole and happy.

But just as her letters went unanswered, her hopes for health went unanswered too.

Catherine picked up the pen and stared at "Dear Sunny," already written on the top of the paper. What could she possibly write that she hadn't already? She could only ask after his well-being and the success of the circus so many times, with never a response in return.

But no matter how many times she told herself to stop caring, she couldn't. Some desperate part of her wanted more than anything to know if he was well. To know if the circus was thriving. To know if he ever found his sister or any of the rest of his family. No matter what he thought of her now, she wanted to know he was all right.

Catherine dropped the fountain pen onto the table, wondering if maybe it was finally time to admit the truth. For the first year, she was able to believe that the letters were being delivered to the wrong place. That somehow the letters could never catch up to the circus's constant tour around the country. But then one year of unanswered letters slipped into two. Then faded into four.

Maybe the circus had moved on and grown to the point where Sunny didn't need to remember one little acrobatic girl the way she needed to cling to the memories to survive.

As tears blurred her vision, Catherine crumpled the paper in her palm and threw it in the direction of the fireplace. It fell short and landed in the middle of the rug, but she didn't bother to rise from her chair to pick it up. She pressed her knuckles to her lips and stared out the window as she tried to wipe his smiling face and his unanswered promises from her memory.

"I'm sorry I'm late, miss." Ruth burst into the room without knocking. "But I have your dinner now."

Catherine straightened in her chair and blinked the tears from her eyes. "It's all right. I hadn't even noticed."

Ruth hustled across the room to bring the tray to Catherine's lap. "We have a lovely roasted quail tonight, with potatoes and carrots. I can bring pudding for dessert in a bit if you have the appetite."

She settled the tray on Catherine's lap and helped arrange the napkin over her dress. As Ruth started to pull back, she gasped. "I forgot to sprinkle on your medication."

"My medication?" Catherine frowned.

"I know Mrs. Combs is the one who administers it, but there was an emergency at the mine. She gave me strict orders to add it to your food. I'm so terribly sorry, miss. I must have forgotten in all of the chaos of packing her dinner and getting her out the door."

Catherine's mind whirled to try to keep up with the maid's rushed words. Medication? Ethel claimed the doctor never gave her medication because there was nothing that could help her wasting disease.

"Where did she leave it?" Catherine asked.

"On the desk in her study, miss. I'll go fetch it right away—"

"No, it's all right. I'll get it and put it on my pudding later, but I won't be ready for that until closer to bedtime. I'm sure taking my medicine an hour or two late won't hurt. Just make sure you don't tell Ethel when she returns. There's no need to make her mad at you when there's been no harm done."

"Thank you, miss." Ruth bobbed into a grateful curtsy.

"I'll ring for you when I'm ready for the pudding," Catherine assured. "Thank you for bringing my dinner."

Ruth bobbed one more curtsy before leaving the room. Catherine poked at her food for several minutes until she was sure she gave the maid time to pass through the hall. Then she set the tray aside and made her way out of the room. Her steps were short and shuffled, and she leaned on the wall for support. With painstaking determination, she made her way down the hall.

Once inside the quiet, dark study, Catherine turned on the electric light and went to the desk. Resting on top was a small vial of fine brown powder. Catherine held the vial up to the light. It must have been the medication, but she didn't know the first thing about pharmaceuticals or how to tell what it was.

She tucked the vial in her skirt pocket before sitting in the chair. One by one she rifled through the desk drawers, looking under and behind everything for more of the mysterious medication. The bottom right drawer refused to open. Perhaps it was simply important documents or valuables, but Catherine's father had installed a safe behind a painting for those.

On a whim, Catherine crossed the room to one of her father's bookshelves. She searched along the shelves until she found two identical books shelved next to each other. Opening the second one proved her hunch. The inside was cut out, leaving the perfect secret nook for a ring of keys. Ethel had no need to create hiding places of her own when Catherine's father had already created plenty.

Catherine returned to the desk with the keys, and the fifth one she tried opened the drawer. Inside she found a mortar and pestle and a small brown bag. She opened the bag, expecting to find pills or herbs.

"Seeds?" Catherine whispered in bewilderment as she stared at the contents.

She emptied several seeds into her palm. They looked like nothing more than apple seeds.

"Catherine, make sure you spit out the seeds," her mother gently chided as they sat under one of the many apple trees that made up their orchard.

"Why?" Catherine wrinkled her nose but obediently spit out the seed she'd bitten off the apple.

"For one, they won't taste very good, but they also aren't good for you. If you eat too many, they can make you sick."

Catherine pulled the vial from her pocket and stared at the brown powder. After pulling out the cork, she sniffed the contents inside. Though faint, she detected an earthy, plant-like smell, and when she sniffed the apple seeds in her palm, the smells matched. Catherine stared at the vial and the seeds, trying to understand what she had stumbled upon.

Abandoning the seeds on the desk, Catherine went to her father's bookshelves again. She searched through any botany book she could find until she finally found a section that addressed the apple seeds. She skimmed over the information, many of the scientific terms going over her head, but near the end she found what she was looking for.

Some believe that avoiding apple seeds is an old wives' tale, but the warnings ring with a bit of truth. Crushing an apple seed will release an inner compound known as cyanogenic glycoside. When hydrolyzed, cyanogenic glycoside becomes the poison known best as cyanide.

Catherine gasped and nearly dropped the book but forced her shaking hands to hold it steady as she finished the paragraph.

However, an individual seed holds very little cyanogenic glycoside, thus rendering a single seed you may ingest virtually harmless.

Catherine closed the book, her gaze drifting to the bag of seeds on the desktop. Perhaps a single seed was harmless, but what about dozens or more, crushed into every meal, every day?

Catherine didn't know the first thing about poisons or their effects, but she had read novels before that used cyanide for various nefarious acts. She could use her imagination to figure out its sole purpose.

She sagged against the bookshelf, her knees growing weak. Ethel was always in charge of her food. Ethel was always in charge of her doctor visits, and often she would draw the doctor away from Catherine to talk to him in private, claiming she didn't want to stress Catherine. Ethel was the one who first admitted to Catherine that she might not live to her twenty-first birthday.

Was that her intention all along?

Catherine clasped a hand over her mouth, and the bookcases seemed to close in on her as her chest tightened. She needed to tell someone. To get help. But who? The staff changed so often she didn't know who could be trusted. Perhaps Ruth could be trusted, but what could she do against Ethel?

Her parents' solicitor popped into her memory. Ethel had no choice but to retain the same solicitor who oversaw the affairs of the estate and mines after Catherine's parents died. It was his job to ensure nothing got in the way of Catherine's legal right to the estate upon coming of age. But how long had it been since she'd seen the man?

The last time Catherine asked to join Ethel in the meeting, Ethel said it was happening at the mines, again so as not to "stress" Catherine. The more she tried to think, the more she realized how completely her guardian had closed her off from any outside help.

For a brief moment, Sunny came to mind, but she banished the thought. If he hadn't responded after almost five years of letters, he wouldn't come to her rescue now.

Numbness washed over Catherine as she crossed the room to the desk. She tried to return everything as she found it, except she kept the vial in her pocket. If Ethel knew she found out about the poison, it might endanger her further.

Not that buying herself time would matter in the end. It was clear Ethel had been trying to steal her future for years, and it didn't look like anything would stop her.

CHAPTER 6

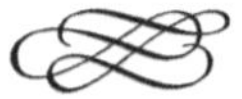

JUNE 1906

Gravel crunched under Sunny's shoes as he followed the curving driveway. The whitewashed stone mansion loomed before him, like a fortress daring him to try to find his way in. He paused at the base of the steps leading to the front door, and he gripped the folded paper in his hand.

Ambrose had warned him this was a bad idea, but he couldn't be this close to her and not even try. He straightened his shoulders and took determined steps up to the front door. He used the gold knocker to make two loud raps.

Only a few seconds passed before a maid in a black dress with a white apron opened the door enough to peer out at him.

"Yes?" she asked, regarding him with furrowed brows.

"Hello." He tipped his chin. "My name is An Sun, and I'm here to call on Catherine Penner."

Her confused expression melted into a frown. "I'm afraid no visitors are allowed for Miss Penner."

His body tensed. *Not allowed?* "Just mention my name to her, and I'm sure she'll see me."

"It doesn't matter who you are. Miss Penner is too ill to receive any visitors."

"Ill? How is she ill?" Sunny didn't realize he had taken a step closer to the door until the maid closed it a few more inches as if to close him out.

"Who did you say you were in relation to Miss Penner?" Her gaze raked him from head to toe without trying to hide her distrust.

Sunny forced his muscles to relax. "I'm an old friend, and if she's ill, it's even more imperative that I get the chance to see her."

The maid pressed her lips in a thin line. "One moment, please."

Instead of inviting him to wait, the maid shut the door in his face. Sunny paced backward on the landing so he could crane his neck and see the upper-level windows. Was that why Snow had never written? He had thought she'd turned her back on them completely, but maybe she'd fallen too ill to reach out.

The door reopened, wider this time, but a formidable woman filled the opening. She stood several inches taller than him, a height difference increased by her heels, and she stared down a narrow, aristocratic nose at him. Her cold, blue eyes narrowed.

"Who are you?" she demanded without any sort of greeting or air of cordiality.

Even if he'd never seen the woman for himself before, Sunny didn't have to guess who she was.

"I already told your maid who I am, and I demand that you allow me to see Snow." Sunny stepped closer to the door again. "Let her decide for herself if she wants to see me."

Recognition dawned in her eyes before a stiff smile lifted the corners of her pink lips. "Ah, I see. You're one of the little miscreants from that circus. *Catherine* wants nothing more to do with that part of her past or the circus that almost ruined her reputation forever. She has moved on, and I think it's time you did too."

She started to move the door, but Sunny put his hand on it to keep her from shutting him out. "I don't believe you."

Anger replaced her smug expression. "Excuse me? I refuse to argue with the likes of you. Get off my property."

Sunny thrust his note in front of her. "Not until you give this to her and let her decide for herself. If you refuse me again, I'll find my own way to her."

The woman stared at the note for a long moment. "If I take this note to her, will you accept her answer and leave?"

"*If* that's her answer, yes. But I will have her answer."

The woman snatched the note, and his hand had scarcely come off the door before she slammed it again.

Sunny crossed his arms as he planted his feet a shoulder's width apart. He hadn't come all this way to be thrown off the property by anyone but Snow herself.

And surely... surely, she wouldn't do that.

Sunny refused to budge from his position in the torturous moments that stretched into minutes, but before he could start to doubt that Ethel would return, the door reopened. The guardian wore her smug expression again as she crossed her arms, wrinkling the frill collar of her gray blouse.

"Catherine cast the note into the fire without even looking at it. What does that tell you?" She lifted a delicate eyebrow.

The air seemed to rush out of Sunny's lungs as if he had fallen from the trapeze onto his back.

"You've had your answer. Leave." She thrust her finger toward the long drive.

Sunny slid one foot back, but his reeling thoughts kept him from turning away. It had to be a lie. Snow wouldn't turn him away without seeing him.

"Do you want me to involve the authorities?" she snapped. "Leave, or I'll see that you're put in irons!"

Those words broke Sunny out of his disbelief. Even though everything in him wanted to stand his ground and fight her further, he knew that getting himself in trouble with the local law would cause the entire circus a headache. Leon would have his hide—regardless of the fact he was on the verge of eighteen and responsible for himself.

Sunny descended the front steps with heavy feet. It had to be a lie. Snow wouldn't be so cold. A million ideas flew through his mind at once. Maybe if he came back after dark... Maybe if he pretended to leave out the front gate and then circled around the back... Was there another way to send word to Snow that didn't involve going through her guardian?

But then a small voice in the back of his mind voiced a question he didn't want to consider. What if her guardian wasn't lying?

Sunny slowed to a stop at the gate and wrapped his hand around one of the iron bars warmed by the sun. What if that message was directly from Snow's lips, and that's why she had never written?

Sunny released his hold on the gate and began to retrace his steps down the dusty road that would eventually lead him back to the field the circus had claimed for the weekend. Not a day had passed that he didn't think about the quiet girl who had turned his world upside down, but maybe the circus was a distant memory she would rather forget. She had barely been with them for two years, after all.

An ache radiated through his chest at the thought, but even as he tried to deny it, the doubt had already taken its hold.

Maybe he was the fool for holding so tightly to such a short part of their history.

CHAPTER 7

OCTOBER 1905

Snow bounced on the toes of her ballet flats, running her hands down the stomach of her leotard. She had managed to pin her hair in a fashionable bun, but in a strange twist of events, it was Byron who helped her apply performance makeup. The clown had colored her lips with red that matched her outfit, and then he had painted around her hazel eyes in a way that made them glitter and pop.

When she had finally turned to the mirror in the costumer's trailer, she caught a glimpse of the graceful performer Sunny saw two days ago. She had stared at her reflection for a few minutes, taking in the young woman who looked nothing like the scrawny girl she knew herself as.

Now Snow peeked through the back curtain of the big top, blowing out a breath. A live band beat out the heart-racing soundtrack to Titus's daring ride around the ring. The crowd came alive with cheers as he backflipped from one horse to another with flawless execution.

Pressing her fingertips to her temples, Snow turned from the curtain and walked a few paces away. Whispering her routine to herself, she began stretching her legs and arms in preparation. With every bang of a cymbal and cheer of the large crowd, her nerves jumped and threw off her stretches. Was this a bigger crowd than normal? Maybe not, but it felt like it.

Maximilien sauntered up to the curtain, his top hat under one arm. That was her sign that it was almost time to mount the trapeze. Snow groaned as she crossed her arms over her stomach, which suddenly threatened to heave.

What if she missed a transition and fell? There was no net this time.

Maximilien's strong stare followed her nervous pacing, but she was too stuck in her panicked thoughts to care. Was it too late to tell Leon she had changed her mind about performing? Sunny knew his own routine well enough to change back to a solo act last minute.

"What are you afraid of?" Maximilien's clipped question snapped her out of her thoughts.

"What?" Snow paused her pacing, the ringmaster's attention doing little to calm her nerves.

"What are you afraid of?" he repeated, his nasally French accent adding a flourishing slur to his words.

She tried to gather her frantic thoughts enough to pull together a response. "I'm afraid of making a mistake. I could get hurt. Or I could hurt Sunny. The crowd will laugh at me. Leon will regret putting me in the act, and I'll embarrass Sunny."

He raised one dark eyebrow. "Have you made a mistake before?"

"Well, yes, so many. That's why I'm so scared—"

"Why are you performing?"

"Because Leon told me I was ready and put me in the lineup. He already had posters made. What if I fail, and he regrets—"

"What does Sunny say?"

Snow clenched her fists, resisting the urge to scurry away from the intimidating man. "Well, I mean, in practice this morning he told me how proud he was of my improvements. He said that practice was my best performance yet, and that it was circus worthy."

A hint of a smile lifted his stern expression, but it disappeared as quickly as it came. "And Leon?"

"He told me two days ago that I was ready to perform, and he hasn't said anything else since."

"Then that is all you need to know." He turned back to the curtain and parted it with two fingers to check the progress of Titus's routine.

Snow opened her mouth to protest, but the words died in her throat. What was she supposed to say to that? "I'm still scared."

Maximilien heaved a sigh as he turned back to her. "You have tried, failed, and learned what not to do. If that isn't enough, Leon does not lie. Nor does he pander to pride. If he says you are ready, you are. Sunny knows the trapeze best of anyone here. If he says you are ready to be a performer, you are. Trust their words, *Petite* Snow. Trust them. You are ready."

Snow fell silent, and he turned back to the tent flap. She stared at his tall form clad in the velvety blue ringmaster suit, complete with two long tails off the coat and shiny black boots that reached his knees. In almost two years of being with the circus, this might have been the most she had ever spoken to the stoic gentleman. As one of the seven founding brothers, he was always around when she was with the others, but she never took the time to get to know him. His ever-present fierce expression, even when relaxing around the fire in the evenings, didn't exactly encourage conversation.

Sunny had shared stories with her about how he and Maximilien clashed in the early days of the circus. They were two polar opposite personalities trying to share the same ring. It only added to her lack of desire to understand the ringmaster.

But now as Snow stood behind him, his confident words settling over her, she remembered the rest of Sunny's stories.

Sunny had also told her about how God had worked on this lifetime performer full of pride and softened Maximilien's hard edges. Sunny mentioned how God had worked on him as well, forcing Sunny to find a new perspective through Maximilien. It had allowed Sunny to see the value in Maximilien's talents as a performer and an excellent organizer of their crazy circus, an invaluable position they couldn't live without.

"Trust their words, Petite Snow. Trust them."

They weren't profound words, but the longer Snow mulled on them, the more she felt the jitters in her stomach stilling. It was a simple answer, but maybe it was enough.

The crowd inside the tent roared to life, whistles and claps ringing out, and her stomach dropped to her slippers again.

"Are you ever afraid?" she blurted as Maximilien settled the top hat over his carefully combed hair.

For the first time outside of the center ring, his lips quirked in a proper smile as he glanced over his shoulder. *"Non.* But my problem has never been feeling too small. This *famille* has a way of making you see yourself as you truly are. They shrunk me." He lifted his flat hand to the height of her head and drew it across the air to his shoulder. His smile widened. "And it seems they have grown you."

The crowd surged to their feet with renewed energy as Titus took his final circle around the ring. He bowed from a standing position on the backs of the two horses. Snow watched through the tent gap with Maximilien, drawing in another deep breath that filled her chest and straightened her spine to her full height.

Maximilien tilted his head to whisper in her ear, "And remember, *Petite* Snow, you do not go in the ring alone."

She smiled, a blush rising on her cheeks. "I know Sunny will be out there with me."

"Oui, but I meant the One who has given you this talent. He goes with you. Never forget that."

With those words, Maximilien slipped past her. Adjusting his top hat and pulling his jacket straight, he advanced toward the ring with long strides as Titus exited to meet his waiting brother. Ambrose greeted the horses with sugar cubes and his brother with a clap on his sweaty back.

In the center of the ring, arms outstretched and voice booming through the tent, Maximilien encouraged the crowd into more hysterics over Titus's performance before seamlessly transitioning to teasing more acts to come. As he talked, Byron traipsed in front of the first row, surprising the children. Laughter rippled through the audience in response to his antics and magic.

Snow looked across the big top to see Sunny slip inside the tent, and before the flap fell closed, she caught a glimpse of Gerard stretching outside the big top. They weren't the only ones with something big planned. His act would follow theirs, and he would be attempting something new.

Even without seeing him, Snow could picture Leon somewhere in the shadows, as he was every performance night, directing stagehands and overseeing the execution of the show. Ready and waiting to use the skills from his past life as a doctor to tend anyone lest they obtain injuries.

The energy of the tent pulsed, seeming to push against the seams of the tent canvas. It was electrifying. When Snow slipped into the tent, every cheer, every drum, every clap reverberated in her chest. As her gaze swept past the swinging lights to see each of the brothers again, a realization settled over her that brought stability to her limbs.

She wanted this.

In less than two years, Snow had come to love this troupe like family, and now they were giving her a chance in the spotlight. It wasn't about escaping the confines of her old life anymore. Even fear couldn't stop her from realizing that she wanted to perform, to make the circus proud, and to be part of their family forever. The dull, meaningless existence that was her life before them had faded like a distant dream.

Snow set her sights on the pole in front of her. The affixed ladder would carry her to the trapeze. With each step forward, her heart echoed those words over and over.

She loved them.

She loved the trapeze.

She wanted to perform.

She wanted *this*.

In the swirling chaos of the big top that whipped her emotions into a flurry, a longing overtook her to give in to the call of hope. History told her hoping was dangerous, but the call was almost too strong to ignore.

What if Sunny and the others were right? What if God brought her here as an answer to all her lonely pleas?

For the first time since losing Chester, the desire to pray overtook Snow, but when she tried to find the right words, everything seemed to fall flat. Perhaps it was appropriate to thank Him for this blessing, but no words seemed sufficient to express the depth of affection she felt for the seven brothers. Some part of her thought she should ask something, but... What more could she ask for? Even if she had something to ask, would God listen to someone who'd denied Him for so long?

At the base of the ladder, Snow paused to peek around the pole in the direction Sunny would be climbing. He must have had the same idea because their gazes connected, and he smiled at her. Her lips formed a returning smile of their own accord, and it remained in place as she ascended the ladder.

God... please let this last forever.

Once at the top, Snow positioned herself at the edge of the rise and locked her eyes on the bar dangling before her. As Maximilien announced their trapeze duo act, she refused to let her gaze dip to the crowd. Instead, she focused beyond the bar to Sunny waiting across the expanse of air. As Maximilien neared the end of his grand introduction and the music swelled, Sunny mouthed a countdown from ten. When his lips formed "one," Maximilien swept his arms toward the platforms and the spotlights swung with him.

Breaking her gaze from Sunny, Snow turned to face the audience and stretched her arms above her head with a delicate raise to her toes, as Sunny had instructed her, complete with a large smile.

With one last deep breath to ground herself in the moment, Snow grasped the bar, and before she could second-guess it, she pushed off from the platform. Her body soared through the air on the momentum of the trapeze. As every muscle strained to arch her body, the repetitious music from the bandstand below matched the beat of her racing heart. For a moment, she and Sunny each did their own tricks on the trapeze, swinging back and forth at an opposite rhythm. Working in the exact timing they'd developed in practice, each new trick brought their momentum in sync until they swung at each other in an even arc.

Halfway across the dizzying void, Snow released her fingers from the trapeze bar. For a brief, heart-stopping moment, she felt nothing but the electric air around her. Then strong hands wrapped around her wrists, anchoring her to safety once more, and she looked up into a smile that made everything else fade. Riding on the rising roar of the crowd, Snow swung in the security of Sunny's grasp. Then she transferred from his hands by hooking her legs over the next waiting bar. The thrill carried her into the next death-defying move with no regard for aching muscles or tiring stamina.

Every fiber of her being glided on the wings of euphoria.

Snow flew through the remainder of their routine on the pulsing adrenaline. She put every ounce of flare and performance ability she could into the movements of her athletic body. Any time her eyes met Sunny's, she felt a surge of strength in her performance. After her final twirling flip through the air, she let the crowd's deafening roar carry her back to the rise. For the first time since taking to the trapeze, Snow dared a glance at the crowd.

A chilling pair of blue eyes stared back at her from the edge of the seats, and everything else faded out of her attention. She missed the timing for a graceful landing and instead stumbled onto the wooden plank. Her attention was forced away from the crowd as she recovered and remembered to dip into a graceful bow.

But the gaze remained tattooed in her mind. There was no doubt. It was Ethel Combs.

∾

SEPTEMBER 1910

"Well then. Goodnight, Catherine."

Catherine remained still in her bed until she heard the door close. She rolled onto her back and stared across her room. Ethel often came to tell her goodnight, but it seemed the real reason all along was to see if Catherine had eaten all of her dinner. Tonight she had, but Ethel never needed to know that the vial had failed to make it into her pudding.

Catherine reached under her pillow and wrapped her fingers around the cold glass cylinder. Perhaps she should destroy it so that Ethel would never know she possessed it, but what if she needed the evidence? As if evidence would do any good when she had no one to take it too.

Or did she?

Catherine sat upright and looked past the end of her bed in search of the crumbled paper she threw hours before. Would Sunny answer her letters if he knew she was in danger? Once upon a time, she believed he would do anything to protect her.

After five years of unanswered letters, it almost seemed above hoping for, but what other hope did she have?

Catherine crawled to the end of her bed to look over the floor near the fireplace, but the crumpled letter was nowhere to be found. Stepping onto the carpeted floor with her bare toes, Catherine looked near the chair and under the bed. Perhaps Ruth realized it was trash and tossed it in the fire when she came to tend it for the night.

Even with that simple explanation, an unsettled feeling poked in Catherine's chest when she climbed back into bed. She tried to roll over to sleep, but slumber evaded her through the night. The aches in her body drove her to toss and turn, and the whirling of her thoughts kept her mind from slipping into the peace of sleep.

A headache numbed her thoughts as morning light peaked through the curtains, but she couldn't find the strength to stir. When Ruth slipped in to stoke the fire, her gaze tracked the maid.

As the maid turned to leave the room, Catherine lowered the covers from her shoulders. "Ruth?" she called hoarsely.

The maid paused in surprise. "I beg your pardon if I woke you, miss."

"No, I was awake." With painstaking efforts, Catherine pushed herself upright. "Last night there was a paper on my floor. Did you throw it in the fire? You're in no trouble if you did. I'd just like to know what became of it."

Ruth frowned before shaking her head. "No, miss. Was it important?"

"Not exactly," Catherine murmured. "Thank you. You may bring my breakfast as soon as it's prepared."

"Yes, miss." Ruth curtsied before leaving the room.

To Catherine's knowledge, the only other person to step foot in her room was Ethel. Was it possible Ethel took it? For what purpose?

Catherine tried not to let the thoughts alarm her as she laid and waited for the maid to bring her breakfast. After Ruth brought the tray to her lap, she picked at the porridge, eating as little as she could to satisfy her empty stomach, but even that small amount was difficult to down with the knowledge of what the porridge may contain.

As soon as Catherine decided she was finished, she forced her tired body from the comfort of the bed. Instead of wasting energy on dressing, she donned her slippers and a silk robe. After checking in the hall for servants or her guardian, she made her way down to her father's study. As she'd hoped, Ethel was still elsewhere, most likely enjoying breakfast in the dining room below.

Catherine shut herself in the quiet peace of the study and began searching her father's shelves. After several minutes of pacing along the length of the wall, scanning the aged spines, she found a small section of medical books. She skimmed through several tables of contents until she found one that talked about poisons and venoms.

As Catherine's shaking fingers flipped the pages to the section on cyanide, her heart hammered with anxiety. Her ears tuned to the door behind her, hoping she would hear any footsteps before her guardian could burst in on her.

With bated breath, Catherine skimmed the section on cyanide. Like the botany book, many of the scientific terms made it difficult for her to comprehend the information, but eventually she found a section on the symptoms of chronic cyanide poisoning.

Her heart dropped as she read the list of endless symptoms she knew well. Tiredness, inability to handle cold, depressed moods, poor memory and concentration, shortness of breath, limb swelling, carpal tunnel, and loss of one's voice. The list went on, but Catherine didn't need any more proof of what her guardian had been doing.

At the sound of footsteps in the hall, Catherine quickly closed the book, and the door opened a moment after she put it back on the shelf.

"What are you doing in here?" Ethel demanded.

Catherine turned to face her guardian, but her trembling knees forced her to lean against the bookcase. "I was trying to pick some reading material for the day. I'm feeling low on energy, and I think I'd like to sit in my room and read."

"If you're tired, you should probably nap." Ethel crossed the room to the desk, her heels clicking on the polished wood floors.

"I think I might. Nothing is sparking my interest." She hesitated as she straightened from the bookcase. "Oh, before I forget, I left a piece of paper on my floor yesterday, but I can't find it now. The maid also doesn't know what happened to it. Did you see it when you came in my room last night?"

Catherine studied Ethel's face, but her frown offered little to be interpreted. "Why did you leave a letter on the floor?"

Catherine's heartbeat roared in her ears like rushing water. *Letter?* "I was going to throw it out, but I've changed my mind. Did you see it?"

"No, I didn't." Ethel turned her attention back to the items on the desk. "Perhaps you did something with it and forgot. This wouldn't be the first time. Maybe you'll remember after you've rested."

"Perhaps so." Catherine shuffled across the room.

Her mind reeled as she retraced her steps to the bedroom. Perhaps her memory was fuzzy at times, but Catherine knew she'd never mentioned that the paper had contained a letter.

Catherine slipped into her room. She leaned against the door, but the walls seemed to lean toward her, pressing in, reminding her of how much this was a prison rather than a home. No way out. No way for anyone to get to her.

She squeezed her eyes shut. Some part of her still didn't

want to believe this crazy plot her guardian was enacting. It seemed too horrible, too unbelievable to be true. But the evidence was mounting.

When Catherine forced her eyes open, her gaze fell on the writing supplies still sitting on the side table. If Ethel was poisoning her, what else had she been sabotaging? There was only one way to find out.

Catherine dropped into the chair and picked up her fountain pen. She straightened a fresh piece of paper on the table.

Dear Sunny,

Even if you've thrown away every letter before this, I beg you to listen to me this once. I need you to keep your promise to never let me go. If you don't, I will fall.

After signing the short letter with her nickname, "Snow," she folded the paper. Like she had done many times before, Catherine sealed it into an envelope and addressed the outside to Sunny at the postal location much of the circus's mail had been sent when she was with them. Then she crossed the room to ring the maid.

"You called, miss?" Ruth peeked in the door a few minutes later.

"Yes, can you please post this letter?" Catherine held out the envelope. "It's imperative you do so immediately."

"Of course, miss. I'll take it straight away." Ruth rushed down the hall. Catherine counted to five before following after the maid, but she kept her steps slow and deliberate so that the girl wouldn't hear her following.

"Where are you going in such a hurry?" Ethel's commanding voice called from the study after the maid flew past the doorway.

"Miss Catherine asked me to see to this letter posthaste," Ruth explained, slowly turning on her heels. Catherine fell into a nearby doorway to remain unnoticed. "I'll be back in a couple of minutes."

"No need for you to take a special trip." Ethel's voice drifted closer to the hall.

"Miss Catherine wanted it posted right away."

"I understand that. I'm leaving for the mines in a few minutes. It will be easier for me to drop it on the way."

Ruth hesitated without responding, but when Catherine dared to peek around the corner, Ruth handed the letter to Ethel.

"Thank you, ma'am."

"Now, I'm sure you have more important chores to attend to." Ethel dismissed her with a flick of her hand.

Ruth scurried off without further delay. As Ethel whirled to go back into the study, Catherine crept down the hall. When she peeked into the study, Ethel stood by the desk, holding the corner of the envelope to the flame of a match. Catherine felt her heart crumbling as Ethel watched the letter burn. Then she dropped it into the fireplace.

Catherine pressed her back to the wall and buried her face in her hands. Sunny had never been ignoring her letters. Did even one of them make it through her guardian's watch?

With heavy footsteps, Catherine made her way down the hall where the portraits of her ancestors stared down at her with harsh gazes. In the long hall with ceilings far above her reach, Catherine had never felt smaller.

No matter what she tried, Catherine would never be able to send word to her circus family. She was completely and utterly alone.

As she slipped into her room, panic squeezed at her lungs and threatened to overwhelm her. Then, like a quiet whisper over her shoulder, a small thought broke through her whirling mind.

"You do not go alone."

Tears rushed into her eyes as she struggled to believe that

small whisper. God had never seemed to notice her before. What would be any different now?

Her guardian had managed to blot out Catherine's existence to the outside world. In her head, Catherine knew Ethel couldn't hide her from God. She'd been raised to understand His omnipresence, but history had wounded her ability to believe.

Even with that knowledge painfully twisting at her heart, the utter loneliness pressing in on Catherine made her desperate.

"God, please," she whispered into the quietness of her room. "If You see me. If You hear me, please send someone to my aid. I don't want to die alone here."

Who else in the world did she have left?

CHAPTER 8

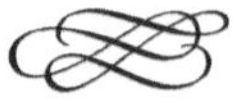

OCTOBER 1905

"Snow!" Sunny's arms enveloped her the moment she stepped through the canvas of the big top.

She hugged him back, but her mind still reeled from what she'd seen. It was Ethel, wasn't it?

She started to pull away, hoping to catch another glimpse of the crowd, but Byron, Titus, and Ambrose were not far behind with hugs of their own. Everyone talked at once about the perfection of her and Sunny's performance.

Snow offered them partial smiles and weak hugs before tearing herself away to go back to the canvas. With trembling fingers, she parted the fabric to peer at the crowd. She scanned the aisle where she'd seen Ethel, but her seat was empty. No matter how many times Snow scraped her gaze across the crowd, Ethel was nowhere to be found.

Was it possible she was mistaken after all? She was too afraid to hope. She had been so sure of what she'd seen.

"Snow, is everything all right?" Sunny asked.

She turned around to find everyone watching her with concern and confusion. With so many eyes trained on her, her chest tightened until she felt like she couldn't draw in another breath.

"Yes, I'm all right," she choked out. "I'm sorry. I thought I saw someone I knew, but I think I was mistaken."

Sunny started to narrow his eyes and open his mouth, but she turned to the others instead. "Thank you so much for your compliments. I did stumble at the end."

"But who could tell?" The strongman snorted. "Everyone was too busy cheering for that magnificent performance. Sunny should have been part of a duo all along."

Ambrose shook his head. "No, he waited for the perfect partner."

Snow gave them a wobbly smile, her eyes misting over. She hoped if anyone else noticed, they would shrug it off as an overwhelming wave of emotion from her first real performance.

Sunny put his arm around her shoulders. "You did amazing, Snow."

She looked into his smile, but she could still see the concern lurking behind his expression. As she leaned into his side, she wished she could tell him what she thought she saw, but the eyes of everyone else prevented her. Instead she gave him the best smile she could muster.

"There will be time for celebration later," Leon broke in. "I believe you'll be on soon, Gerard?"

"Yes, sir." Gerard gave a stiff salute, the rippling of his muscles causing the tattoos on his bare arm to dance. Then he turned on his heels to step through the canvas.

The others dispersed to their tasks at hand, but drawn like a moth to a lantern, Snow drifted back to the tent flap. No matter how many times she scanned the crowd without seeing Ethel, she had to look again. It couldn't have been her imagination. A shiver of fear ran through her body as the cold gaze surfaced in her memory.

The canvas lifted away from her fingers, and she glanced up

in surprise to see Sunny's arm extended, holding it back for her. "Are you still trying to take it all in?"

She couldn't meet his eyes, so she turned her attention back to the big top. A "yes" lodged on her tongue, but she couldn't lie to him. Sunny would see right through her.

Sunny said nothing, his steady hand keeping the canvas parted for her viewing. His arm bumped her shoulder as he held it up, and the heat of his body hovered behind her. She leaned back into the comfort of his presence a fraction of an inch.

No matter how hard she tried to keep her gaze fixed on Gerard carrying a bench full of audience girls around the main ring, her eyes kept darting back to the crowd like she expected Ethel to materialize at any moment.

"What is it, Snow?" Sunny whispered in her ear, causing her to jump.

"I-I..." She scanned the crowd one more time. "I'm just..."

"Did you see someone?" He hesitated. "Did you see her?"

She looked into his perceptive gaze. She didn't know how, but he knew. Her tongue stuck to the roof of her mouth. She mustered a small nod. His mouth drew into a straight, grim line.

Sunny took her hand, intertwining his tan, slender fingers with hers. He pressed their knotted hands to his chest. The sequins on his deep red shirt winked at her in the light of the big top. "I won't let you go, Snow. You're safe with me."

Snow searched his deep brown eyes, a lump forming in her throat at the sincerity she found. As they returned their focus to the ongoing show, his strong grasp overshadowed the fear that filled her mind. The rough callouses on his palm pressed against her skin, bringing a measure of comfort. Those calloused hands had gripped hers at the perfect moment in their performance, saving her from falling thirty feet to the ground. Every day in practice she'd learned to trust those hands. They would always keep her from falling as long as she did her part to let go and reach for them. He would never let her fall.

Neither of them moved until the grand performances concluded. As the last performers stepped out of the ring, Sunny let the tent canvas fall back into place, but he didn't release her hand. They turned together to greet the other performers.

The buzzing noise of the crowd spilled from the big top as they flooded the circus grounds. The performers withdrew behind their tents for privacy so they could revel in the night and burn off excess adrenaline with laughter and stories. Eventually, they would all have to shed their stage clothes and begin the tedious act of cleaning up after the circusgoers, but in the meantime, they could celebrate another show well done.

Praise rained from all around Snow, and she did what was expected of her—she relayed the feeling of being in the air above an adoring crowd. However, her mind remained preoccupied, a pair of eyes always lurking in her memory.

Sunny seemed to have no problem joining in the laughter and the stories around their nightly campfire, but he never left her side, even without her asking. As they sat on a hay bale by the fire, he held her fingers loosely between his, and Snow didn't miss the raised eyebrows from the other brothers.

Titus whispered something in his brother's ear that sent them both snickering, but Snow chose to ignore it when Ambrose wiggled his eyebrows at her.

After the embers of the fire died, Sunny walked Snow to her tent. He stopped in front of it to face her in the moonlight. He pressed a kiss to her cheek, sending a rush of heat into her face.

"I'm proud of you, Snow. You executed a beautiful performance tonight. I knew you were ready for the big top."

"I couldn't have done it without you," she admitted.

He grinned. "We make a great team. Good night, Snow, and happy sixteenth birthday."

He squeezed her hand before releasing it and turning in the direction of his tent. Snow bit her lip with a smile as she watched him go. In the midst of the overwhelming events of the evening, she had completely forgotten it was her birthday, but she knew this would be her favorite birthday ever.

Snow turned to go into her tent, but light caught her eye several yards away. It leaked out of the shuttered windows of the wagon that Leon called his "office." She paused, wondering why he was in his office that late at night, but the longer she thought on it, the more she realized he hadn't been at the bonfires with everyone else.

Had there been a problem after the circus ended that no one else noticed? It wouldn't be the first time some unruly or complaining circusgoer caused a problem he had to tend to. Not everyone could be a happy customer, even at the circus. Argumentative performers were prone to causing problems too. Whatever issue had pulled Leon into his office, Snow knew word would be all around camp by morning. This drama would be part of the morning news across the campground along with the fact Sunny had held her hand all throughout the bonfire.

As Snow stepped into her tent, someone emerged from the wagon, but it wasn't Leon. Snow gasped and snapped her tent closed before Ethel could see her. Her body trembled as she peeked out. Ethel stalked across the campgrounds, lifting her skirts high above the dust. An automobile with a canopy top waited near the road, and the driver popped out long enough to open the back door for Ethel. After spinning thin tires in the dirt, the vehicle took off from the circus.

Snow remained frozen in place, her mind whirling. There was no doubt now Leon knew who she truly was and where she came from. Would he send her back? Should she run before they could find her? But Ethel had left without her. Was it possible Leon would be willing to protect her? At sixteen, she was legally Ethel's ward, but maybe a court of law would still listen to her preference if she fought hard enough with the brothers on her side.

Leon left the wagon, but a minute later, he returned with Sunny on his heels. Tension radiated from both men. Unable to deny her curiosity, Snow stole through the darkness to the wagon. She knelt near the window and tried to listen to their voices through the thin walls and drafty window.

"What do you know about her past?" Leon asked with an edge in his voice that Snow had never heard before. Chills ran up and down her spine. After a moment of silence, Leon slammed his hand on something wooden, and she imagined it was the crate he used as a desk. "An Sun, so help me, this is not the time for you to learn how to keep a secret."

"She made me promise I wouldn't tell," Sunny declared without a waver in his tone. "And I won't break my word to her. What happened?"

Leon took a deep breath. "According to Ethel Combs, Snow's full name is Catherine Penner, heiress to the Penner mining company and their entire estate." After a moment more of Sunny's silence, he went on. "Mrs. Combs, her guardian, has demanded we return Snow to her at once."

"You can't!" Sunny snapped, making Snow jump. "I can't tell you why, but you must never let that woman get her hands on Snow."

"I don't like the way she handled the situation. I can only guess why you're acting so strongly, but there's more to consider than that. I managed to buy us time until morning to make a decision, but she's already leveling threats at the entire circus if we don't surrender Snow."

Sunny snorted. "Let her threaten all she wants. You know your own lawyers, don't you?"

"I doubt we have a chance against Snow's legal guardian. She threatened us all, but the reason I came to you first is because Mrs. Combs had a few choice threats for you particularly." Leon sighed. "She claims remaining with the circus will ruin Snow's reputation and the future her parents tried to ensure for her.

She says if we insist on ruining Snow's reputation, she will ruin ours. Starting with you. The things she claims she's capable of accusing you of will prevent you from ever being able to perform in front of a crowd again, if not imprison you."

Sunny let out a choked sound of protest. "Let her spew whatever worthless threats she wants, but Leon, you have to listen to me. Snow needs to stay with us for however long she wants, or until she's legally of age."

"If you're sure you want to fight this battle, then we can try to proceed forward. We should warn the others, and maybe by putting our seven heads together, we can come up with a solution that won't endanger us or Snow."

As Leon's voice drifted toward the entrance, Snow scrambled away from the wagon. She darted back to her tent before they could discover her spying. Sinking onto her cot, she hugged herself to try to stop shaking.

Snow wanted nothing more than to stay with the circus and have the brothers fight for her, but at what cost? She couldn't let any of them ruin their lives to protect hers, not after everything they'd done for her. Especially Sunny.

She buried her face into her hands as the swirling emotions overwhelmed her senses. Snow wanted to cry, but the tears refused to come. She wanted to scream in anger, but the sound lodged in her throat.

She should have known. She should have expected it. For her, all good things always came to a premature end.

~

SEPTEMBER 1910

Catherine paced in her father's study while waiting for her parents' solicitor. She had telegrammed the solicitor, requesting he meet her personally. She had waited until Ethel left the house to send Ruth on the errand this time. Surely the man in charge of overseeing the affairs of her parents' estate would be able to help her against her murderous guardian, but it had been over an hour since she'd asked him to meet her. What if her guardian returned home before he arrived?

After she sent Ruth off with the telegram, Catherine had considered forgetting her plan and running away instead. She could have packed a bag and run out the door before anyone stopped her.

But how well had that worked six years ago? She had nowhere to go, and Ethel would always find her. Besides, she barely had the strength to leave her room, let alone leave home.

Unable to take the suspense of waiting, Catherine snuck out of the study. Watching down the hall for any servants, she made her way to the stairs to watch out the front door for the solicitor or Ethel. Halfway down the stairs, voices drifted out of the drawing room, and she froze midstep.

"Her health appears to be holding out longer than any of us expected." The cold tone of Ethel's words chilled Catherine to the bone. Why was she home already? "However, she's not in her right mind. She is always forgetting and doesn't think things through anymore. Is there any room in her parents' will for someone to remain the primary caretaker of the estate on her behalf if she is unfit?"

Catherine sucked in a breath as she recognized the deep voice of her parents' solicitor as he replied, "The will simply stated everything would fall to her on her twenty-first birthday. There wasn't even a stipulation for if she was to marry. However, I suppose she herself could sign authority over to someone else upon taking control of the estate. Is her mind idle enough for you to convince her of something like that? It goes without saying she must do it voluntarily and not under duress."

"I imagine the signing over of the estate would also need to be done in the sight of a witness, such as yourself," Ethel mused.

"Yes, of course."

"That will make things easier."

Catherine gripped the banister as hot anger dropped on her chest. What parts of her life had Ethel not stolen? Ethel stole her health, her letters, and now it seemed she had swayed Catherine's solicitor.

She crept further down the stairs to listen, careful to avoid the third step from the bottom that always creaked.

"I ought to warn you," the solicitor said, "it will be tragic when the young heiress passes away like her parents and her guardian before her. No doubt it will raise suspicion, and if I'm the sole witness to her signing the estate over to you, the authorities may come to me first."

Ethel heaved a sigh. "I will ensure it's worth your time to remain loyal to one of your longest-standing clients. We can haggle certain amounts when the time comes. In return, I'm expecting complete discretion as always."

"Of course, of course. Though it should go without saying that explaining a rockslide as an accident is much easier than explaining sudden poor health in a young woman. Compensation should match the work required."

Catherine's mind reeled at the implication of the solicitor's words. Rockslide? He couldn't mean...

"And I will take care of it," Ethel hissed. "Don't try to blackmail me in my own home. I can ruin you with some knowledge of my own."

The solicitor let out a nervous chuckle. "I meant no harm. I wanted to make sure we were understanding each other, and I see we are. Now, should I go see Ms. Penner for pretenses, or...?"

"Just leave. After a nap, she won't even remember she sent for you."

Catherine knew she needed to go back upstairs before they spotted her, but she couldn't move her feet as the solicitor stepped into the entry hall. His gaze flickered over her before he did a double take and froze. He shot an alarmed look over his shoulder as Ethel stepped out behind him.

Ethel narrowed her eyes at Catherine before addressing the solicitor. "Leave." Her chilling tone left little room for argument.

The frightened man couldn't scurry out the front door fast enough.

"You—" Catherine started, but Ethel marched up the stairs and grabbed her arm. "Let go of me! You're hurting me!"

Ethel ignored her cries as she dragged Catherine up the stairs and across the hall. Throwing open the study door, Ethel shoved Catherine inside before slamming the door behind them both.

"I heard everything." The force of Catherine's words grated on her weak voice. "I know your entire plan, and I will never sign my estate over to you, no matter how ill I am."

Ethel laughed, but it was void of any warmth. "You think so?"

"I know everything you've been doing, and I won't let you get away with it. I don't care what you try to do to me. I'll never stop trying to expose you for who you really are." Catherine's courage mounted with every word, and she refused to back down, putting a chair between herself and Ethel's murderous looks.

"You always thought you were so smart and special, but you know nothing." Ethel sauntered over to the desk, her calm demeanor unaffected by Catherine's threats.

Catherine paused, trying to put together the final pieces that Ethel's talk with the solicitor had revealed. "You've been after my parents' estate since the beginning. Rockslide... You murdered Chester, your own husband."

Ethel made no reply, and she didn't even bother to look shocked by the accusation as she pulled her green dress suit jacket straight and smoothed her hands over the A-line skirt.

"Chester was a good man, and you murdered him." Catherine's voice cracked with emotion. "Just so you could take control. Just so you could take what was never meant to be yours."

"I wouldn't be so sure of that, little Catherine dear." Ethel infused a mocking tone into her voice, tilting her head as her ice-blue eyes assessed her charge. "I'm taking back what was always meant to be mine, and I have been working at it for over nine years. If you think you can stop me now, you might want to reconsider."

"Over nine years? My parents were..." Her voice trailed off. "The carriage..."

Ethel simply raised her eyebrows.

Catherine swallowed as tears misted her vision. "My parents? You took my parents from me too?"

"If you promise to sign the estate over to me on your twenty-first birthday, I give you my word that I'll care for you like a daughter for the remainder of your days. You'll never want for anything. Your life will remain as comfortable as it is now. The public never need know anything other than I was a loving guardian who dutifully cared for her charge until the very end."

Catherine's knees couldn't hold out any longer. She sank into the leather chair, but she shook her head at Ethel's words. "I will tell everyone. I'll tell the world what you've stolen from me."

"And how do you plan to do that? Who will you tell? Who will believe the ramblings of a sick, near-death girl?"

"My health will get better," Catherine promised.

Ethel shook her head with an amused smile. "You have no control of that, and you know it."

Catherine stared at Ethel, but she found no sympathy or care in her expression. "So I'll be the end of your schemes."

"Such a shame that a cherub little girl should have to meet an early end, but I suppose that is life." Ethel crossed the room and rested her cold fingers against Catherine's cheek.

She cringed away from her guardian's touch. "You said this should have been yours, but it never was."

"It would have been had your father married the right woman, but like most foolish males, his head was turned by your mother's beauty. And of course, the fates had to taunt me by making you a spitting image of her, but in time, everything will be set to right again."

Catherine slouched into the comforting folds of the leather chair, trying to understand the meaning of Ethel's words. Every pain she had ever experienced in her life was because Ethel was jealous of her mother? As she stared up at her guardian, she saw the monstrous look in her eyes. How could the monster of jealousy grow so strong?

Ethel grabbed Catherine's arms and dragged her to her feet. "Look at you, poor thing. You look exhausted. You really should rest."

Ethel's iron grip gave Catherine no option other than to walk from the study. Catherine stumbled to keep up with her long stride, still too stunned to say anything further. Her mind scrambled for any ideas to stop Ethel before it was too late, but who could she go to? Where could she escape that Ethel would never find her?

"I'll have tea sent in a couple of hours," Ethel promised before shutting the door.

Catherine reached for the knob, but the lock clicked into place. She sank against the door as her strength completely left her.

All of her worst memories, all of her darkest moments. Every time she'd blamed God for taking anything good from her.

It was Ethel all along.

CHAPTER 9

OCTOBER 1905

now sat on the edge of the rise. She stared off, lost in thought. How could she stand to let her beloved new family put themselves in danger for her?

But how could she bear to leave?

"I knew I would find you here."

Snow blinked down at the tattooed strongman standing beneath the trapeze rise, his neck craned back to stare at her.

"Everyone is searching for you," Gerard called up.

"I-I'm sorry. I wanted somewhere to think." She moved to stand, but he motioned for her to stay.

He started up the ladder that led to the platform, and his weight jostled the entire pole. She clutched the edge of the wood.

When Gerard planted his feet on the rise, he kept a hand on the pole as his gaze darted everywhere but down. "Sunny comes up here to think. So I had a hunch that you might also. I don't know why he didn't think of it first."

Snow faced forward again. "I suppose Leon told everybody about my guardian."

Gerard inched closer before sitting behind her. "Yes. He told us that your guardian is determined to have you back, but Sunny told us you wouldn't want to go. Is that true?"

"I don't want to endanger the circus by staying."

"That's not what I asked."

Snow glanced over her shoulder at him. His hulking form took up most of the platform as he crossed his legs. His shirtless vest showed off the rippling, vein-covered mass of his muscles, decorated in endless tattoo ink, but Snow knew how to look past the intimidating persona to the compassion filling his brown eyes.

Even now, all Snow could think of was the time he used the strength in his massive arms to carry her like a babe to Leon after she took her first major fall in training. As Leon's unofficial medical assistant, his hands—almost as big as her head— were gentle and his deep voice full of kindness while he worked with Leon to treat her minor injuries.

"I know how much this troupe can come to mean to a person," Gerard commented, pulling Snow back to the present and the problem at hand. "I was once a lone sailor who believed his very existence didn't matter, but Leon, Sunny, and all of the others showed me that I was loved and I had a purpose." He paused as a smile spread under his thick mustache. "I still can't believe I say I'm loved. I would have scoffed at the idea a few years ago. The words never would have left my mouth."

"Legally I belong to my guardian."

"Guardianship can be changed." Gerard cocked his head. "Answer honestly. Do you want to stay?"

"More than I've ever wanted anything before," she said.

"Then you will stay."

"Ethel will—"

"One of the first things I learned about Leon was that he will stop at nothing to protect those under his care, which includes you now, and Sunny is as loyal as they come. Those two alone would be enough to make sure your guardian can't take you away, but you don't have only those two. You have seven of us behind you."

Snow stared down at the dark center ring, the straw scrambled and bare in places from the various acts that trod it hours prior. The stands sat empty. The spotlights drooped dark on their stands. Even though everything looked much different than her moment in the spotlight, Snow could remember the feeling that had overwhelmed her. The feeling that this was all she wanted, to perform and stay with the circus forever. No matter how hard she tried to dwell on that memory, the fear of bringing harm to those she'd come to love overshadowed it.

Gerard rested a large hand on her shoulder. "We are family, Snow, and family is unafraid to lay down everything for each other. You don't have to fear your guardian anymore."

Snow looked up into his compassionate gaze again. They were her family. She didn't need Gerard to tell her that. The seven brothers would do anything for her. Sunny would keep his promise to never let her go.

Why wasn't that enough to release the fear in her chest?

"Would you stay if you knew your presence put all of the others in danger?"

Gerard pressed his lips together in answer to her whispered question. A flicker passed over his expression, followed by his telling silence.

"We'll protect you, Snow."

"Snow? Gerard?"

Snow closed her eyes before turning to peer down at Sunny. He stood in the ring, his head tilted back to squint up at them. Her heart squeezed at the worry etched across his tan face.

"Hang on, Sunny. I'll trade places with you." Gerard stood as gingerly as he'd sat, and then he inched his way backward to the ladder.

Snow rubbed her face, turning her eyes to the peak of the big top. Even though his weight didn't jostle the pole like

Gerard's, Snow was all too aware when Sunny stepped onto the platform. His soft footsteps came up behind her, but before she could gather the courage to face him, his arms enveloped her. Giving into the gravitational pull, she twisted around to return the embrace.

He said nothing as they held each other, and she buried her face in the shoulder of his performance shirt. She breathed in the familiar scent of hay, woodsmoke, and something she could only recognize as *Sunny*.

"I'm never going to let you go, Snow," he whispered into her ear.

She tightened her hold on him as her throat ached with restrained emotion. Try as she might, she couldn't stop the tears that leaked from the corner of her eyes. In the center of his embrace, Snow could believe every one of his words. She could trust the same strength he had used to pull her onto that train platform almost two years ago. She could trust the strength that saved her every day in practice. She could trust the same strength that had carried her through the air in their performance hours before.

But Sunny couldn't stop the threats Ethel was leveling at him with his bare hands. His strength wouldn't be enough this time.

"She's going to try to ruin you," Snow murmured into the fabric of his shirt.

"Let her try." A shiver ran down her back at the growl in his tone.

She pulled back enough to look into his determined face. The shadows of the big top highlighted the hard angles of his fierce expression. Snow realized just how much he'd grown since he'd pulled her aboard the circus train. They both had.

Sunny was stronger. He kept his black hair slicked into a respectable, trimmed style, like most of the other men in the circus, instead of the boyish, loose style that used to hang over his forehead. His voice didn't crack nearly as often as it did those first couple of months after she'd joined the circus. With this protective look on his face, she could see every bit of the man he was becoming.

He held her gaze as they remained locked in each other's arms on the small platform. His breath tickled her cheek, stirring the hair behind her ear.

"I don't want to let you go either." She held tighter to his performance shirt.

"Snow..." The warm sensation of his breath erupted goosebumps on her skin. His eyes dipped to her lips, and she wondered if he could feel her heart racing in her chest. His gaze roamed up to her eyes again as if searching for something, and she raised her chin in response. Her eyes fluttered shut as he eliminated the gap between them. His lips collided with hers before softening into a gentle kiss.

A tear slipped down Snow's cheek before she could stop it, but as Sunny pulled back, he wiped it away with his thumb.

"Everything's going to be okay," he promised.

Snow found herself too choked with emotion to respond, and she bit her lip as more tears blurred her vision. How was it possible for her heart to be so full yet ache so much at the same time?

Gerard's words haunted the back of her mind. *Family is unafraid to lay down everything for each other.*

She looked into Sunny's eyes again. It was undeniable that he would keep his word to fight for her, but she knew Ethel would fight too. And Ethel was a woman who always got what she wanted.

Her breath shuddered.

"We have until morning to come up with a plan." Sunny stepped back, but he took hold of her hand. "Let's go join the others."

As he turned to the ladder, Snow found her feet rooted in

place. He paused when their arms grew taunt, shooting her a confused look over his shoulder.

Snow pulled her fingers from the security of his grasp. "Can you go without me?"

He frowned as he turned back to her.

"I have one more prayer I need to pray."

Sunny nodded slowly, the worry remaining fixed on his face. "We'll be waiting."

As he descended the ladder, Snow turned around on the platform again. Through tears, she watched him cross the big top and disappear out the tent flap. She turned her eyes heavenward as the tears dripped down her cheeks.

God, are You listening to me? Her mind screamed a deafening roar toward heaven even if the words never left her lips. *If You brought me here, why are You taking my good gift away? How could You bring this to me just to rip it away? Where is Your goodness in that?*

Snow furiously wiped at the moisture on her cheeks as her prayers fell away in the empty tent. In the replying silence, her heart settled on the only answer she could be sure of. Before she could dwell on the decision any longer, she went down the ladder. When she slipped out of the same tent flap as Sunny, she jumped in surprise at the sight of Gerard waiting off to the side of the entrance. His gaze swept over her expression before he crossed his massive arms.

She dropped her gaze to the grass. "I-I need to get something from my tent real quick. You can catch up with the others in Leon's office."

When he didn't respond, she dared to glance at him, but his grim expression was unmoving.

"Don't make a stupid decision." His deep voice took on a gruff tone.

She cringed at the harshness of his words, but it sparked a bit of defiance in her chest. "You never answered my question earlier." She forced herself to her full height, refusing to shrink again. "Would you stay?"

He worked his jaw back and forth, his steely gaze unwavering. "It wouldn't be the first time I've made a stupid decision."

Snow turned away, unable to stand still under his scrutiny. She shook her head as she started marching away.

"Everyone who ever abandoned Sunny thought they were doing it for his own good," Gerald called behind her. "His father. His brother. Don't add to the number."

She paused, remembering Sunny's brief explanation of his family a few days ago.

"Snow, you have at least seven reasons to stay. We all want you, but if that's not good enough, at least stay for him. Don't leave him too."

An unbearable ache grew in her chest like a fist digging into her heart. None of them understood what Ethel was capable of. Snow met Gerard's eyes again, and he held her gaze, his face firm.

"Please tell him I'm sorry," she whimpered.

Before she could give herself more time to consider, Snow turned on her heels again and broke into a sprint.

"Snow!" Gerard shouted behind her, but she never heard his footsteps pursuing.

As soon as she darted into her tent, Snow began stripping off the beautiful leotard. She tried not to let herself dwell on the fact she had only worn it once, but she also knew she would never forget that one magical performance.

She tossed through the trunk of clothes Leon had provided her until she found the stolen set of boys' clothes she'd arrived in. She forced the pants over her womanly hips, the hems falling short on her shins. The cuffs of the shirt failed to reach her wrists, too, but Snow refused to leave with anything she hadn't come with. She wouldn't steal from the brothers.

As she pulled her original shoes from the trunk, a fabric

flower fell out. She picked it up, twisting it between her fingers as she remembered the day Byron had given it to her. The day he'd dared her to dream. If only she'd known then how completely this circus would change her life.

Snow tucked the flower into her waistband before bending to pull on the tight shoes. After carefully laying the glittering leotard across her cot, she forced herself to leave the tent. She set her sights on the road beyond the little circus camp and made her strides long and determined. She wouldn't—she couldn't—give herself time to second-guess her decision. She couldn't give Gerard enough time to alert the others either.

But when her shoes hit the dirt road, she froze as if by some outside force. Unable to resist the gravitational pull any longer, she cast a glance over her shoulder. Through the maze of tents, she could still see Leon's office wagon. Light leaked from the shuttered windows, and she could picture the seven brothers gathered together within the walls like they had been gathered in the train car the day she arrived.

This time she didn't fight the tears as she followed the dirt road leading to the nearest town. Their seven faces remained emblazoned on her memory, but Sunny's face shone the clearest. As she wiped at the moisture on her cheeks, Snow wanted to scream at God for letting her down again, but what good would more anger do to Someone who never listened? And this time she had nothing else to cling to. She couldn't hope in Sunny. She couldn't hope in the circus.

Sobs wracked her frame as her feet stumbled on the uneven road.

SEPTEMBER 1910

Catherine lay awake in her dark room, the fatigue seeping into her bones. No matter how much she tried to pick at her food, she could tell Ethel had managed to up the dosage of poison. Life seemed to be draining from her body by the day. Ethel was determined to not let her reach her twenty-first birthday after all.

A soft knock sounded on the door before a maid pushed it open. The unfamiliar girl carried a tray over to Catherine's bed.

"Your breakfast, miss." She set the tray on the edge of the bed and hesitated, as if unsure what to do next.

Catherine flicked her hand to the nightstand by the bed, and the maid dutifully moved the tray there. "What is your name?" she asked, her voice hoarse and foreign even to her own ears.

The maid blinked for a moment as if she didn't expect that question. "Mary, miss."

Catherine pushed herself upright, and when the maid stepped forward to help, she waved her off. "Is my guardian home?"

"No, miss. She already left for the mines today."

Catherine nodded. "I suppose Ruth no longer works here?"

"Who?"

Catherine closed her eyes before reaching for the nightstand. It took most of her feeble strength to pull open the drawer. A letter rested next to a faded fabric flower, and she drew the letter out, leaving the drawer open.

"Listen carefully," Catherine whispered. "This letter must reach its intended recipient."

The maid's curious gaze flickered to the name "Sunny" written on the front, and she shot Catherine a quizzical look.

"Do not stop to do anything else. Do not tell anyone where you are going. Go out the back servants' entrance and let nothing stop you until you reach the post office." She pressed the letter into the maid's hands. "Please."

The maid took the letter, shifting nervously on her feet.

"Please come back to me when you return so I know you were successful."

"Yes, miss." The maid bowed before fleeing the room.

Catherine sank back on her pillows. She knew full well that there was a strong chance the maid wouldn't succeed, but she desperately prayed for God's deliverance—that is, if He wasn't finished with her after the anger she had held against Him for so long.

It was too late for anyone to save her. Ethel's plan was going to succeed, but Catherine couldn't bear the thought of Sunny never knowing the truth. For almost five years, she thought she had been explaining herself to him, and he'd chosen not to respond. But now she knew.

Even if it changed little, Catherine had poured everything she could into that letter. She told Sunny why she left, how their memory had never been far from her mind in the almost five years since, and how even though her guardian was going to kill her, she still remembered the hope the circus had filled her life with.

Her gaze drifted to the breakfast waiting on the nightstand. Which part contained the poison? The eggs? The yogurt? The juice? All of it?

"God knew what He was doing by bringing you here. He knew you needed us."

Catherine let her gaze blur out as the memories swept her into the days of yesteryear. Despite the fog in her mind, the memories had been coming easier. She'd spent the last few days since she accepted her fate doing nothing but remembering.

It was like she was seeing her history in clear view for the first time. When she truly considered the events of the past, she found evidence of Ethel lurking. Plotting. Twisting the tragedies of Catherine's life. She couldn't blame anything on a terrible accident or even an uncaring God. Ethel had been manipulating Catherine's life from the moment Chester and Ethel had stepped foot on her parents' estate when she was a girl.

Catherine pulled the fabric flower from the nightstand and twirled it between her fingers, staring at the faded petals.

With her true enemy exposed, the hard anger she'd grown accustomed to—aimed at a God she thought had abandoned her—seemed to fizzle out like a hot coal in a bucket of water. As she shifted through the shattered memories, Catherine discovered the opposite of what her anger had led her to believe. Every time Ethel had attempted to kill and destroy, something or someone new had come to Catherine, keeping an ember of hope alive in her soul to encourage her forward.

God had never once abandoned her.

Catherine swallowed the lump of emotion in her throat. It seemed too much to hope for a future now, but even if Ethel's plan succeeded, she would be sending Catherine to a far better existence, wouldn't she? One free of pain and surrounded by the loved ones she had mourned over for years. Maybe that would be God's final gift to her, if He would truly be so compassionate. Chester had always told her He was, when she chose to repent and believe.

Catherine gripped the fabric flower in her left hand so she could pick up the fork in her other. She started eating the food, as much as her turned stomach would allow. Her eyes misted as she forced herself to keep chewing and swallowing.

Lord, please receive my spirit. Forgive me for turning away from You, but please don't forsake me now.

Her mind grew fuzzy the more she ate, but she kept the image of the seven brothers at the front of her memory. They were the only ones she was leaving behind in this world, but someday she would see them again too. It was a reunion she would earnestly wait for.

God, please don't let me go.

Despite the physical pain in her body and the heavy ache weighing her heart, an odd measure of peace seemed to settle over Catherine. An unexplainable warmth blanketed her chilled limbs.

He was with her.

Take care of them until I can see them again.

CHAPTER 10

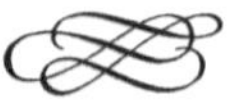

SEPTEMBER 1910

Sunny threw pants and shirts into a carpetbag without paying attention to what articles of clothing he was grabbing. Urgency scrambled his thoughts, hindering his ability to think through what he needed to do.

"What's your plan?" Ambrose asked. He stood near the opening of their tent, arms crossed and feet braced.

Sunny paused his frantic packing and squeezed his eyes shut as he tried to clear his head. "I don't know. Knock down the front door. Climb a wall and sneak through a window. I don't know, but this time no one will be able to stop me from turning that mansion upside down to find her."

Sunny swept up his shaving supplies and hair pomade and unceremoniously dropped them into his bag.

"Right. A solid plan, then," Ambrose muttered under his breath.

Sunny gripped the opening of the carpetbag as his gaze swept the tent for anything else he might need. Why was he even taking the time to pack? A change of clothes or the ability to shave didn't matter with Snow's life hanging in the balance. He scraped his fingers through his disheveled hair, trying to force a deep breath into his lungs. It had been a full week since the letter was postmarked. So much could have happened to her in seven days.

Even if he got a train as soon as he reached the station, Sunny wouldn't be to her estate until morning. Assuming he could find a train bound for Charleston at all, and this close to nightfall.

"I've got to go." Sunny snapped the bag shut. "Tell the others... I don't know. Tell them where I'm going, and I'll—"

"What's this about Snow in danger?" Leon's booming voice announced him before he burst into the tent. "What's this about a letter?"

"Sunny, I thought you could use backup," Titus explained from behind Leon.

Byron, Maximilien, and Gerard crowded into the tent as well, stooping to all fit in the small space.

"Read it for yourself." Sunny tossed the envelope at Leon as he hefted his bag.

Leon opened the letter, and his eyes rapidly skimmed over the contents.

Sunny stepped toward the entrance. "I'll send a telegram once I've gotten Snow to safety, but I don't know how long it'll be before I come back."

"Not so fast," Leon warned.

Gerard grabbed Sunny's shoulder in response to Leon's command. Sunny jerked out of the strongman's grasp, thrusting a finger at Leon.

"Don't try to stop me," Sunny snapped. "I should have tried harder to see her the last time I went to her estate. She wouldn't be in this position if I'd just tried harder. If I'd taken the time to find another way in."

Leon knocked his accusing hand away. "I wasn't going to tell you not to go. I was going to say that you're not going alone." His gaze swept across the other brothers. "Snow told Sunny that her guardian has been poisoning her. Apparently, Ethel Combs was behind the death of her parents and Ethel's husband too. She intends to steal Snow's estate."

Gerard muttered something under his breath, and even Byron looked ready to murder, his face growing scarlet.

"We'll all go," Titus agreed. "Let that witch try to stop all seven of us."

"But there's a show tonight," Sunny argued. "Our show can do without me for one night, but we don't have time to wait until after the performance to leave."

Maximilien raised his eyebrows, stroking one side of his mustache between his thumb and index finger. "We shall just have to tell the other performers that the show must go on, with or without us."

"If Snow has been poisoned, it seems to me you need someone with the medical knowledge to help her." Leon gave Sunny a pointed look.

Ambrose put his hand on Sunny's shoulder. "Don't do this alone."

Sunny spun to exit the tent. "So what's our plan of attack?"

"What was *your* plan?" Leon asked, on his heels.

"I didn't have one yet. I was going to figure it out on the way."

"Sounds like a solid plan. Let's go get our girl." Leon jammed the letter back into its envelope and tossed it at Sunny.

Sunny shoved it into his pocket as the other brothers branched off to grab their own things. Leon headed to the big top where most of the other circus performers were preparing for the show, no doubt to inform them of the change of itinerary.

Sunny stopped in the center of the circus camp, gripping the carpetbag handle in both hands. He tried to slow his racing thoughts.

Hang on, Snow. We're coming. Just hold on.

CHAPTER 11

*L*ight played across Catherine's face as she gazed up through the leaves dancing on the breeze. She blinked around at the apple orchard she found herself in. The limbs of the trees bent to the earth, heavy with bright red apples ready for the harvest. The sweet scent of fallen fruit mingled with the scent of trees and soil, reminding Catherine of years in her youth spent picking these apples every fall.

She reached for the nearest branch, but movement caught her peripheral vision. She looked around the tree and spotted a black horse moving through the rows. The horse drew nearer until it entered the lane she stood on. As the horse emerged from the orchard, its rider came into Catherine's view. Chester sat tall on the horse's back, a crooked smile lighting his freckled face. He used two fingers to doff his black hat.

She stared in shock, unable to believe her eyes. "Chester?"

He glanced over his shoulder, away from her, before urging the horse forward.

"Chester, wait!" She took a step toward them.

He shook his head at her, which made her stop in place. With a wink, he nodded his chin to whatever had caught his attention. Her gaze landed on two figures at the end of the row that she'd failed to notice before.

Catherine blinked several times in disbelief. Her mother stood in a dark green cotton dress covered in a white apron, the outfit she often wore for apple picking. Her black curls escaped the chignon at the base of her neck to tickle her face in the breeze. Her father stood, feet planted apart, the buttons on his brown suit jacket undone so he could hook his thumbs in his suspenders. They both smiled in her direction.

"Mama, Papa." Catherine blinked again, trying to bring their hazy faces into focus. Chester and his horse had disappeared in the trees, leaving her full attention on her parents.

Her father's lips moved, but his voice failed to reach her.

"Hang on, Papa. I'm coming." She seized her skirts to run, but her feet seemed to be weighed down with each step. Fixing her eyes on her parents, she tried to walk faster, forcing each leg forward. But the more she walked, the longer the lane seemed to stretch. No matter how hard she tried, she couldn't close the distance between them.

Catherine stopped, frustrated tears blurring her vision. "Mama, Papa!" she screamed, her hoarse voice choking in her scratchy throat. Her arms ached to hug them and never let go. Her heart burned to kiss their cheeks and whisper in their ears that she loved them. As they watched her stop walking, their smiles saddened.

The familiar aches of her body filled her senses. Her joints moaned with fatigue. She swayed, willing herself to remain upright. This must be the end. Catherine knew it had to be, but that brought more tears to her eyes. She didn't want to die alone. Why couldn't she reach her parents? Even if it was a phantom of her dying mind, she wanted to be held by them as she took her last breath.

But their forms grew hazier until they were a blur of colors at the edge of her vision.

"Please don't leave me alone," she tried to call, but her voice faded as if in a void instead of in the open orchard. The trees dissolved, and she sobbed as she crumbled to the ground, the weight of her own body too much for her to stand.

She lifted her eyes to catch one last glimpse of her parents. "I love you."

～

SEPTEMBER 1910

Sunny waited behind the two police officers as they knocked on the door for a second time. Every muscle in his body tensed, ready to pounce the moment that tall door opened. A strong sense of déjà vu plagued him waiting on the steps of the white-washed stone mansion, but this time he wouldn't leave until he saw Snow.

Finally, a servant opened the front door but stepped back, startled at the sight of the officers and the seven men behind them.

"Pardon for the early intrusion, but is Ethel Combs or Catherine Penner here at the moment?" one of the officers inquired.

"Yes, Mrs. Combs is eating her breakfast. May I ask what brings you here this morning?"

"That's something we'd like to discuss with Mrs. Combs herself, if you please."

"Yes, of course. One moment." The servant scurried away without inviting them in.

Sunny eyed the door left ajar, but Leon rested a hand on his shoulder as if he could read his thoughts. Sunny released a long breath through his nostrils. It had been Leon's idea to enlist the help of the police. It seemed like a sound plan at the time, a plan that would better their chances of successfully rescuing Snow.

However, after two hours spent in the police station trying to convince the officers that the letter was real and she was in danger, Sunny was tired of wasting time.

Ethel Combs came to the door, and she stared down her nose at the officers much in the same fashion she had at Sunny the first time he'd come. Sunny curled his fingers into fists.

"What is the meaning of this, officers?" Ethel demanded curtly. Her eyes narrowed when she noticed the others behind them. "What are these men doing here? I want all of them off my property this instant!"

The two officers traded a glance before addressing her. "We're here to investigate a concern about a Miss Catherine Penner who resides here."

"I don't know what these carnies have told you—" she began, but Sunny couldn't hold himself back.

"Where is she? I know you have her locked in there somewhere. She told me everything you've done to her." Sunny started up the steps, but Leon and Gerard grabbed his arms before he could get far.

"Let the police handle it," Leon hissed in his ear.

The officer who seemed to be taking control of the situation shot Sunny a warning look. "There's no need to make this more than it needs to be. We simply want to check on Miss Penner and her well-being. It's our understanding she's been ill for some time?"

"Ill, yes. A wasting disease for which there is no cure, I'm afraid. I've been doing my best to keep the poor dear comfortable for whatever time she has left." Ethel lifted her chin, her sharp blue eyes daring Sunny to try something again.

"It's not a wasting disease," Sunny growled. "It's poison!"

Anger snapped in her eyes, and she inhaled sharply. "The only ones posing a danger to her are these men. They're the ones who lured her away in the dead of night years ago to join their freak show, and ever since Catherine broke free of them, they've been trying to steal her back."

"Those are nothing but filthy lies," Ambrose burst.

The other brothers shouted their own protests as Ethel raised her voice to argue back. The two officers split, one to push back the brothers and the other to place a hand on Ethel.

"Quiet!" the leading officer barked. "Clearly there is a difference in accounts here. I believe the best way to settle this is to hear from Miss Penner herself. Mrs. Combs, where is she?"

Ethel stiffened, her pink lips pressed in a harsh line. After several seconds, she finally answered, "Catherine isn't fit to leave her room. All of this ruckus would do nothing but harm her condition further. If you wish to know the truth of her condition, I could fetch her personal doctor who has seen to her from the onset of this ghastly illness."

"I would rather speak to her before we disturb the doctor." The officer stepped toward the front door.

"She's unfit for company," Ethel protested. "Do you wish to hasten her death? The poor girl has done nothing but suffer since the death of her parents. Let her rest in peace."

Sunny's anger boiled almost to the point of rage. No amount of concerned words could mask the coldness in Ethel's voice. Surely the officers could see through her lies.

"I'm afraid we've been as kind as we can be," the officer declared. "Move aside, Mrs. Combs. We'll see to Miss Penner ourselves."

"I forbid you from entering this house!" Ethel straightened to her full height, filling the doorway the best she could.

"You no longer have a say in the matter." The two officers each grabbed one of her arms and pulled her from the doorway. She stumbled forward with shrieks of protest.

Sunny couldn't wait for the officers to gain control of the writhing woman. He ripped away from Leon and Gerard while they were distracted, and before anyone could grab him again, he bound up the stone steps and through the doorway.

The entryway opened in three directions: a hall to the right, another to the left, and a grand staircase draped in red carpet straight ahead. A cluster of servants filled the left hallway. Sunny whirled to them as protests followed behind him, some from Ethel and others from the officers.

"Where is Sno—" He closed his eyes as he bit down on the familiar name, and he willed her real name to surface on his tongue as his mind stalled. "Catherine. Miss Penner. Where is her room?"

The gaggle of servants pointed wordlessly at the staircase, eyes wide.

Sunny took the stairs two, then three, at a time. Footsteps pounded behind him, but he didn't bother to look over his shoulder to see if it was his brothers or the police or curious servants.

At the top of the stairs, he began to open any door he found. The brothers came along behind him, helping search the long hall. Each empty bedroom, office, or sitting room fed the adrenaline pumping through Sunny's muscles. Five years of wondering and heartache channeled his focus into one purpose.

Sunny came to a set of double doors near the end of a long hall protected by the stares of somber portraits. When he tried the doorknob, it refused to yield to his touch.

"Snow!" He pounded his fist on the wood. "Snow, are you in there?" He pressed his ear to the door, but if there was any sound within, he couldn't hear it over the wild beating of his own heart.

"Sir, I can help."

Sunny spun on his heels to see a young woman dressed in the black-and-white maid uniform. Before he could respond, she disappeared into a door down the hall. In the time it took him to make two strides after her, she reappeared in the doorway.

"I pray you're not too late." Her eyes were wide with concern as she stretched out her palm. "Are you Sunny?"

He reached for the key in her hand but hesitated at the mention of his name. "Yes. Is she...?"

"No one has been allowed in her room for several days." The maid gulped. "But I'm the one who mailed that letter for her. I'm glad you came."

Sunny nodded in response before whirling back to the locked door. His fingers trembled as he shoved the key into the lock. When he finally spilled into the room, darkness met him. Long gray curtains held back whatever remained of the day's dying light, and it took a moment for Sunny's eyes to adjust enough to notice the four-poster bed in the center of the east wall.

Sunny's rapid breaths stopped at the sight of a still form draped in a faded quilt. One of his feet slid forward as if on its own accord, but everything else in him tensed. The form was too still. Too small.

I pray you're not too late. The maid's haunting words rattled in his mind.

Sunny forced a breath into his lungs with each step he took until he reached the edge of the bed. The light from the open door provided him enough visibility to see the form on the mattress.

She wasn't much more than that. A mere form. Small, bony. Pale beyond recognition. A wisp. An apparition. Her black hair spilled across the pillows, the only contrast between her face and the white bedding.

"Snow," Sunny whispered into the still quiet of the room. "Snow, I came."

Tears blurred his vision as he reached for her sunken cheek.

His finger hovered above her skin before making hesitant contact. Her paper-thin skin was cool to the touch.

He sagged into the mattress as his knees gave out, and he cupped her cheek in his palm. "Oh God, please no." He desperately smoothed her hair away from her forehead, his gaze raking over her body for any sign of life. "Snow, it's me. Please wake up."

"Sunny." Leon blocked most of the light from the door.

"Did you find Miss Penner?" An officer pushed around Leon into the room.

Sunny took hold of her delicate hand. "She's here."

"Is she...?" The officer drifted closer, staring down at her still form.

Leon stooped next to Sunny, and someone else turned on the electric lights Sunny had failed to notice in the room. He squeezed his eyes shut, unable to face the full reality of what they'd found.

"Yes." Leon drew the word out. "Yes, she is still here."

Sunny's eyes flew open, and he searched Leon's face for the truth.

Leon's eyes grew red as his fingers sought the pulse in her neck. "Barely, but she's still here."

Sunny gripped her limp hand as he searched for signs of life. When he stilled and waited, he caught sight of what he'd failed to see in the darkness: the smallest rise and fall of her chest, so slow it was easy to miss.

Even the officer seemed to breathe a sigh of relief. "We'll have a doctor fetched right away. What poisoning did she claim Mrs. Combs used?"

"There's no need," Leon stated. "I'm a doctor, and I came prepared. Gerard, my ba—"

Before he could finish, the strongman hurried forward and thrust Leon's black bag into his hand.

"We'll bring her back, Sunny." Leon set the bag on the nightstand and began rifling through it. "I have the sodium nitrite to counteract the cyanide, if Snow was correct about the poison. We'll bring her back."

While Leon worked, the officer turned on his heel and left the room. Down the hall, he barked orders to officially place Mrs. Combs under arrest. The rest of the brothers crowded into the room, coming to circle the bed. Byron removed his bowler and touched her knee, eyes glistening.

Sunny returned his focus to Snow. He pressed his lips to her knuckles, tears burning his eyes. "We're here, Snow, and you're going to be okay. I promise."

CHAPTER 12

SEPTEMBER 1910

Catherine's eyes flickered open, but it took her eyes a moment to adjust to the dim lighting. Her bedroom's ornate ceiling stretched high above where she lay on her soft bed, and the gray curtains remained drawn over the windows, allowing the smallest sliver of light through.

Had Ethel failed again? Catherine squeezed her eyes shut as an ache ripped through her chest. She hadn't wanted Ethel to fail. She wanted to return to whatever unconscious state managed to bring her face-to-face with those she loved most.

Her parents. Chester. Then somewhere in the murky darkness, she'd heard the voices of Sunny, Leon, and Gerard. Why couldn't she stay in that blissful land of the in-between?

When Catherine tried to lift her hand to wipe away her tears, a weight kept it anchored against the bed. She turned her head to find a man resting his head on the mattress, his tan hand eclipsing her ghostly white skin. She stared at the back of his black hair, trying to decipher if this was reality or a dream.

"Sunny?" Her voice was the same raspy wisp she'd grown accustomed to.

The man stirred with a grunt and lifted his head. The grogginess immediately faded from his eyes as he bolted upright. "You're awake!" A familiar smile lit his face.

"Sunny." She struggled to bring her fuzzy thoughts into focus to comprehend what was happening. Was she dreaming? Hallucinating? His hand in hers certainly felt real, but then again, so had the smell of the orchard.

"How are you feeling? Do you need a drink? Something to eat?"

She blinked as his fast words bombarded her sluggish thoughts. "Am I not dead?"

The smile fell from his face, pain darkening his eyes. "Thank the Lord, no. When we busted in, I thought for sure we were too late."

She licked her dry lips as her thoughts finally began to take logical form. Her letter had made it past her guardian. God had answered her prayers for deliverance. "You came."

"Of course I came." He swallowed as several emotions rolled over his face before settling on something akin to regret. "I wish I had come sooner. I wish I had..." He stopped as his voice cracked. She gave his hand as much of a squeeze as she could muster. "I'm just happy to see you awake."

Before he could say anything more, the bedroom door opened, and Leon slipped inside. His eyes lit up when he saw Catherine smiling back at him. More silver than black dominated his unfashionably long beard and hair, but he still wore his hair tied back like she remembered.

"You're awake." His eyes crinkled with his smile in a way she didn't remember. Had five years been a lifetime for them too?

She managed a weak nod. "I suppose I am."

He approached the bed. "How do you feel, my dear?"

"Still weak, but..." She hesitated as she tried to take full inventory of her body. "Better than I have been in a long time. My thoughts are clearing the longer I'm awake. Where is Ethel? How did you get past her?"

"Shh. Don't strain yourself." Leon raised a hand to feel her forehead. Then he used the stethoscope draped around his neck to listen to her heart and lungs. "You won't have to worry about Ethel ever again. Your letter saw to that, and I do believe you're on the mend. Thank the Lord."

Catherine looked to Sunny for further explanation, but his eyes were trained on the mattress. He worked his jaw back and forth. She sought out his hand again, and the moment her fingers brushed his palm, he held fast to her hand.

"We're all here." Sunny cleared his throat to rid his voice of a husky mask. "The others are around here somewhere too. We all came as soon as we got your letter."

Catherine laid her head back against her pillow, closing her eyes as exhaustion pulled at her consciousness again. "I'm so happy to see you. I can't believe you're here. I tried to write so many times. Ethel... She stopped them all. She was behind everything." Her words choked in her throat as tears rushed to her eyes. "My parents—"

Sunny gave her hand a gentle squeeze. "I know. I read the whole letter, and now so have the police. She'll pay for everything she did to you."

A tear slipped out of her closed eyes and raced down her cheek. Raw pain burned in Catherine's chest even as the rest of her body seemed to relax at the knowledge that her struggle was over. Nothing the law could do to Ethel would bring back everything she took from Catherine, but at least she could take no more.

"You keep resting and regaining your strength," Leon murmured. "Take your time to heal. We're not going anywhere."

She cracked open her heavy eyes to look up at him again. "Thank you, Leon."

He bent to kiss the top of her head, then clapped Sunny on the shoulder before slipping from the room again.

Catherine turned her focus to Sunny. "I'm so sorry for

leaving without saying anything." She licked her dry lips. "I just wanted to protect you. I wouldn't have been able to live with myself if I brought harm upon you all. I tried to write to you to explain. I tried to reach out. I truly did. Ethel just—"

Sunny squeezed her hand to stop her. "You don't have to explain. I always understood, but all of that is in the past now. Please just do what Leon said and rest. You need it."

Catherine tried to resist the fatigue. "But I've just begun to have you back."

"I'll be right here when you wake." He raised her hand to his lips and brushed a kiss on her knuckles.

Her eyes were already shutting on their own accord, but she fought to keep his face in focus. "Promise you won't let go?"

"I promise."

Catherine surrendered to the irresistible pull of slumber, but she relished Sunny's hand in hers as long as she could. His strong, calloused hand. At least for a moment, that was all she needed.

OCTOBER 1910

"And she promised to write," Sunny said, leaning forward in the chair at Catherine's bedside. He rested his elbows on his knees.

Catherine pushed her finished dinner tray away as she listened to him talk about seeing his sister for the first time in years. In the few days since she'd woken up, Sunny had kept her company every moment he could. They had used the time to reconnect, mostly with him telling her about everything that had happened at the circus in her absence.

"I'm so glad you had a chance to see her," Catherine said.

Sunny nodded. "I've felt like there's been a weight lifted off my shoulders ever since."

Warmth filled Catherine's core at the thought of him reuniting with his sister and receiving the forgiveness he'd craved for so long. She slid her hand toward him on the mattress, and without a word exchanged, he slipped his fingers into hers.

They sat in comfortable silence for a few minutes. Sunny's thumb brushed over her knuckles in a soothing pattern.

"Snow, reconciling with my sister was wonderful, but nothing has felt right at the circus since you left," Sunny spoke up. "I've felt like something was missing."

"I'm sorry," she murmured.

"You did what you had to, but even when I tried to find other trapeze partners, no one felt as right as you did."

Her heart warmed. "Sunny, I can't even begin to express how much I missed you."

Sunny leaned forward, capturing her gaze in his. "I—"

Before he could finish, the bedroom door swung open wider, and the six other brothers marched into the room with grins. Leon stepped to the front of the group with a chocolate cake on a platter. A single candle burned in the center of the frosting.

"Happy birthday, Snow!" the six brothers bellowed in unison.

Her eyes widened as she sat up taller against her pillows. "Birthday? It's my birthday? I didn't even realize."

Leon brought the cake to her bedside and held it in front of her. "Make a wish."

Catherine laughed. "What more could I wish for?" She glanced around at the seven faces clustered near her. "I have you all back."

"There has to be something," Ambrose insisted as he leaned against one of the posts of her bed. "Even if it's something simple like a new hat."

A smile danced across her lips, and she stared into the flame.

Maybe she didn't quite believe in the power of a wish made on a candle, but she knew exactly what she wanted.

Lord, I wish for this moment to last forever.

When Catherine blew out the flame, the brothers cheered, and Leon transferred the cake to her nightstand for cutting. Gerard brought forward the plates.

"I'm sure you already realize this, but now that you're twenty-one, your parents' estate is officially yours," Leon commented as he handed her a slice of cake. "We'll have to seek out a new solicitor soon since your old one is dealing with some legal problems of his own."

Catherine froze. She knew what turning twenty-one meant. She'd always known, but somehow, in the haze of the last few days, that part had slipped her mind. Everything was hers.

"H-has he been found?" she stammered before shoving a bite of cake in her mouth.

"I received word that the police caught up to him last night at the train station."

Catherine's gaze flickered to Sunny for his reaction, but he kept his eyes lowered even as he accepted the cake. He sliced off a small portion with his fork and nibbled on it.

In all of their conversations over the last few days, they'd avoided one topic: the future. He'd never asked, and she'd avoided thinking about it. Catherine knew it would complicate things in a way she wasn't ready for.

"I wonder if the mines are still operating without my guardian," Catherine commented.

"I've spoken with one of the managers, and he's making sure business continues as usual until you say differently," Leon assured.

"And we have been interrogating—" Maximilien began, but Titus interrupted him with a snort.

"More like interviewing. You make it sound like we've been handling them like we're police."

Maximilien shot him a glare. "Interrogating and interviewing are the same, *non*? We have been interrogating your staff. We will not release anyone without your consent, but we want to make sure there is no one loyal to *Madame* Combs who could do you harm."

"Thank you," Catherine cut in. "There's so much to do. So much I have to attend to."

"It can all wait a day or two more." Leon gave her a warning look with lowered brows. "Until you've fully recovered your strength."

She blew out a breath, but she didn't argue the point further. She had a feeling it would take a long time to recover her strength, but even still, she knew she wasn't quite ready to handle running the estate and mines.

As Catherine finished her piece of cake and the brothers talked around her, she couldn't stop her thoughts from returning to the future decisions she needed to make. She wondered if Sunny's silence was evidence that he was considering it too.

Somehow, in the last few days she'd made the subconscious assumption that she would return to the circus and everything would go back to what it had once been. Why did she think it would be that easy? She was no longer the young girl with no connections who could run away to the circus. Leaving meant sacrificing her claim to her parents' legacy.

An ache filled Catherine's chest at the thought. As much as she loved her circus family—more than life itself—she still dearly loved her parents too. They had poured their entire lives into ensuring this estate and their coal business would thrive long after they were gone, as generations of Penners had done before them. How could she abandon that?

Catherine rubbed her forehead as the swirling thoughts made her mind ache.

"Snow." Leon pulled her from her thoughts. "I didn't mean to sour your birthday."

"But it is something I need to think about, and soon." Catherine scraped the tip of her fork through the moist crumbs on her plate.

"Soon, but not today. As your doctor, I order you to continue on your complete rest and enjoy the remainder of your birthday." He smiled.

"But when the time comes to deal with it, will you help me find a new solicitor? I trust your judgment."

His eyebrows flickered upward in surprise. "Of course. I'd be honored."

Gerard started collecting the empty plates even as Titus went back for a second slice, and conversation resumed again. Catherine sought out Sunny's hand, and when she took hold of it, his gaze met hers. She tightened her hold, and he seemed to understand the silent plea because he returned it by giving her hand a squeeze.

She tried to focus on the joy of being in the presence of her circus family again, but the weight of the decisions before her pressed at the back of her mind.

CHAPTER 13

OCTOBER 1910

Catherine gazed through the glass door at the orchard behind her family's sprawling mansion. The landscape before her seemed to be another blissful dream, but this time she knew she didn't have to wake from it.

Leon, Gerald, and Maximilien sat at the lawn table and chairs in the shade of the house, engaged in a card game. Smoke from Maximilien's cigar ringed their heads like a halo. Byron was in a nearby chair with a separate deck of cards, fanning and flipping them with magical movements.

Whoops and hollers drew her attention to the rows of apple trees, where she spotted Ambrose and Titus racing her family's horses. Drawing her crocheted shawl tighter around her slim shoulders, Catherine stepped out into the beautiful autumn afternoon. She paused to take a deep breath of fresh air ripe with sweet apples and rich earth. It was everything she'd longed to enjoy for some time, and now there was no one to keep her imprisoned inside her own home.

"Hello, Snow," Leon called as he approached her. "How did your meeting go?"

Catherine released a slow breath. "I liked this solicitor. He listened to my interests for the estate, and he had some wonderful ideas for how to proceed." Her gaze scanned the orchard as she spoke, seeking out the one brother she had yet to see.

Her gaze snagged on a lone figure clad in a gray suit, strolling through the trees. It was strange to see him in a proper suit, with shoes on too.

"That's good to hear." Leon's gaze followed hers. "Sunny has been anxiously awaiting news from your meeting as well."

"Excuse me then." She brushed her hand over Leon's arm before descending the patio steps.

Her heart seemed to flip in her chest as she approached the orchard. With her skirts in hand, Catherine strolled down the lane between the trees. Spots of sunlight filtered through red and yellow leaves to kiss her face, and a light breeze teased small hairs from her bun. Goosebumps rippled across her arms beneath her cream, cotton blouse.

When a twig snapped under her shoe, Sunny glanced over his shoulder. A smile spread over his lips, crinkling his eyes at the corners, and her heart did a second flip. She quickened her pace to eliminate the gap between them.

"You must be feeling better to venture all the way out here," Sunny commented, his gaze roaming her face. "The sunlight looks good on you."

She smiled, slipping her hand in his offered elbow. "I couldn't stand another moment trapped inside."

"And how did your meeting go? Any better than the last one?" He led her forward at a slow, steady pace.

"Much better. This solicitor saw my vision and knew the best way to execute my ideas. So I think he won himself the job." She studied Sunny's profile as she spoke, but he kept his gaze forward, his face unreadable.

Silence enveloped them, and she felt the same tension that had popped up more than once between them in the last few days. It always came when they broached the topics of her future and her parents' estate. Those conversations never lasted long since Sunny often fell silent, but the tension was always palpable. She could feel the restrained questions he kept to himself, probably so as not to pressure Catherine into a decision she wasn't ready to make. Until this afternoon, she had no answers to offer anyway.

"I think he'll be the perfect man to assist me moving forward," she declared.

Sunny cleared his throat. "So you've decided what you want to do with your estate, then?"

"Yes." She stopped walking, forcing him to stop too.

He turned slowly to face her when her hand slipped from his arm. His gaze searched her face, worry lines etched between his brows.

"My parents' estate is a legacy passed down through the generations of our family, and I want to make sure their legacy continues."

His Adam's apple bobbed as he swallowed.

Catherine couldn't stop a smile from inching up her lips. "My new solicitor is going to help me find a trustworthy manager to take care of the estate and mining company so that I'm free to return to my circus family without worry."

His eyes widened in surprise. "You're coming back?"

She nodded. "If you'll have me, but I know—"

"Snow! Of course we'll have you!" He snatched her up to twirl her in a circle.

She laughed and wrapped her arms around his neck. "Wait, wait! I wasn't finished!"

He returned her to her feet but kept his arms around her. "I had been hoping, but I knew how much your parents' legacy meant to you."

She cupped his face in her hands. "Yes, it means the world to me, but you are the only family I have left on this earth." Her smile died as she took a deep breath. "But there's still another important discussion we need to have."

"About what?" He frowned.

As the words stuck in her throat, Catherine reminded herself how clearly God had revealed Himself to her in the last few days. In every twist of her hard life, He was there, and He would see her through the future, too, no matter the uncertainties that remained.

"It's about my position with the circus." She rested her hands on Sunny's arms, hoping he wouldn't let her go too soon. "I don't know if I'll ever be able to take to the trapeze again. Ethel took all of my strength, and I'm not as young as I once was. I don't know if I can ever regain what she stole."

Sunny rested his forehead against hers, forcing her to meet his eyes. "You learned it once, and I have no doubt you'll be able to again."

"You don't know that," she whispered.

"We won't know until we try, and we will try. If for some reason you can't regain your strength, we'll find another purpose for you. You belong with us, Snow."

Warm tears misted her vision. "I know, and this time there won't be anything to tear me away. I'm here to stay."

"Promise you won't let go this time?" His soft breath tickled her face.

"I promise."

Her eyes fluttered shut as Sunny closed the gap between them. As his lips captured hers, her heart pounded in her ears with a familiar rushing euphoria. *Thank You, God.*

A whoop behind them drew her from the blissful moment. Wind whipped at her skirts and hair when Ambrose and Titus raced past on their horses. She peeked around Sunny to see Titus riding backward, clapping as he continued to holler at them.

"Ladies and gentlemen, the greatest trapeze duo of the twentieth century has made their return!" His loud declaration drew the attention of the other brothers. "Give it up for the high-flying duo!"

Catherine buried her face in Sunny's shoulder, her cheeks burning. Sunny's chest rumbled with laughter. As more cheers and claps drifted from the direction of the patio, she kept her face buried in his suit jacket, the short hairs on the back of his neck tickling her fingers. Beneath the burning embarrassment, a prayer of thanksgiving rose from deep in Catherine's spirit.

The events of the last five years lingered in the weakness of her limbs and in her memory like a bad dream, but the promise of tomorrow filled her lungs with fresh air. The uncertainty of the future couldn't taint her moment of joy. God had answered her desperate pleas in what should have been her last moments, and she knew He wouldn't leave her now.

What more did she have to fear from the future?

EPILOGUE

MAY 1912

*E*ven thirty feet above the earth, the energy thrumming through the tent swelled to ignite the anticipation in Sunny's chest. The cheers of the crowd drowned out the booming words of Maximilien below, and performers decked in a dazzling array of colors and fabrics exited the ring to allow full attention on the aerial act. Sunny knew better than to look at the size of the crowd, not that the swinging spotlights would have allowed him the opportunity. He didn't need to see them to feel the weight of a thousand eyes on him.

Squaring his shoulders, he turned his attention to the platform on the other side of the big top tent. His fiancée waited for him across the expanse of air. He flashed her a smile that beckoned her to leave the platform and fly.

And she did.

Sunny took to his own trapeze, and even though he tried to focus on his part of the routine, he couldn't stop himself from stealing a glance in her direction. The repetitious music from the bandstand below matched the beat of his racing heart, and he watched her graceful body arc without missing a beat. Halfway across the dizzying void, she released her fingers from the trapeze bar. For a brief, heart-stopping moment, she fell through the electric air.

Then, at the climax of the song, Sunny wrapped his fingers around her wrists, anchoring her to safety once more, and she looked up with a smile that made everything else fade away. Riding on the rising roar of the crowd, he swung with her in the security of his grasp. Only once her legs hooked over the next waiting bar did he release his hold, and thrill carried him into their next sequence of death-defying moves with no regard for aching muscles or tiring stamina.

Every fiber of his being glided on the wings of euphoria that he thought he'd never share with her again.

Sunny flew through the remainder of their routine on the pulsing adrenaline. When he dared to glance at Snow, she was putting every ounce of flare and performance ability into each move of her restored body. When their eyes met, he felt a surge of strength in his own performance. After his final flip through the air, he let the deafening roar of the crowd carry him back to the rise.

When he had mounted the wooden platform, he bowed to the ecstatic crowd. Then he turned to catch Snow's gaze across the expanse. He returned her smile with an uncontainable grin that held a future's worth of promises.

Snow let the joy swell in her chest as the crowd surged to their feet in a thunderous applause. She was home.

ACKNOWLEDGMENTS

My goal after publishing *Before the Ever After* was to put another story into the hands of readers in less than a year, but I never would have achieved that goal without the love and support of you, the readers. I want to start by thanking you for taking the time to pick up my little story, and a special thank you to everyone who already read my first. Your support enables me to keep going in this dream career of mine.

But this story would not have made it into print if it wasn't for several important people who helped me along the way.

I want to thank all of my alpha readers who read an unpolished story and offered feedback. Thank you to Brooke, Ellana, and Brian. Each of your unique perspectives helped me to see areas that needed improvement that I wouldn't have found on my own.

Thank you also to my beta reader, Korin. Your love of my first novella touched me deeply, and I was excited to have you as part of my team to polish this one. Thank you for taking time to read this little novella and offer feedback!

Thank you to my line editor, Caitlin Miller. Your edits gave my prose the improvement it needed, and your sweet comments helped me believe even more in this story!

Thank you to my proofreader, Megan Gerig. You've been an enthusiastic reader of my stories for too many years to count, and now to have you as an official proofreader of my novella meant the world to me. Above all, thank you for believing in my writing!

I can't go without thanking my parents, whose love and support and help has allowed me to continue on this journey as an author.

Last but never least, I thank God for this call He placed on my heart, for the imagination He has colored my days with, and for the courage He gives me when I start to doubt my ability to bring these stories to life. I write for the enjoyment of story and for the love of crafting characters, but I ultimately do it all for His glory.

Soli Deo Gloria

BEFORE
THE EVER
AFTER

CHAPTER ONE

$\mathcal{A}$s Evelyn's eyes flickered open to take in the early morning light, visions of colorful silks and lace twirled through her thoughts. Couples danced across a polished floor beneath large electrical chandeliers. Every inch of her skin tingled with the memory of strong but gentle hands resting on her waist. Piercing blue eyes captivated hers as they stepped in time to the live orchestra, but when she blinked, she was staring at the wooden beams stretched across her peaked ceiling. She would have believed it to be an enchanting dream if not for the leftover nervous excitement still quivering in her belly.

Drawing herself upright, Evelyn dared to peek past the end of her bed. The discarded pile of light blue chiffon and satin on her wooden floors was a sure reminder that every blissful moment was, in fact, a memory. She flopped back on her pillow, her chest deflating with a deep sigh.

A brief, electrifying kiss under a floral trellis seared into her thoughts, and heat flooded her cheeks. Burying her face in her hands, she turned into her pillow to let out a girlish squeal. Daniel Prindall, heir of a million-dollar factory enterprise and frequenter of her daydreams since girlhood, had kissed her, little Evelyn Macaree from 24th Street.

She lay still in her bed for several minutes, letting more memories of the night wash over her—memories she wanted to relive every second of every day so she would never forget them. The live music reverberating through the tall, arching ceilings, filling the room with life and energy. Daniel assigning himself the position by her side for most of the evening, doting on her with plenty of refreshments between their dances. The gazes of the other girls along the wall, their whispers following them in wonder of who she was, and for one night, she was someone else entirely.

As the sun drifted upward in the sky, the light jabbed into her eyes too brightly to ignore. She dragged herself upright again, casting one last wistful glance at her gown on the floor. The feeling of pure bliss that made her chest swell with ecstasy faded away, leaving behind a gaping ache at the thought of the fairytale night evaporating into mere reminiscence forever.

Evelyn climbed out of bed to gather the dress into her arms, tendrils of the perfume she had worn the night before escaping from the folds of the fabric to offer her one last tangible reminder of the night. After opening the lid of the trunk at the end of the bed, she folded the dress with care on top of the other garments tucked inside. She would have to return the dress to her friend Edith whenever the chance arose, along with an enormous thank you for the outfit and the evening.

A pair of heels lay abandoned on the floor, but when she picked them up, she paused to run her thumb over the scuffs caused by her hasty climb up the lattice to her window. For the first time, a bit of guilt pricked at her chest. Never before had she so blatantly gone against her stepmother's wishes, but with all of the wonderful memories, she could only feel guilty about it for a second. There was no good reason for her stepmother to forbid her from attending the party other than pure jealousy that Edith had invited Evelyn to such a prominent function.

After closing the trunk to conceal the only evidence of her disobedience, she focused on getting around for the day. The simple, worn wool of the skirt she pulled on paled in comparison to the luxurious feel of the satin against her skin, and the pleated gray blouse covered her ghostly collarbones that had seen the light of day for the first time in her life.

She sighed as she sat in the broken dining chair that served as a vanity chair. Staring past the rust spots on the aging mirror, she pinned her dark waves into a conservative bun on top of her head. She paused with hairpins clasped between her lips as more memories of the night surfaced. The way Edith had curled and arranged Evelyn's dark tresses resembled the Greek goddess statues in the Prindall's grand entryway. Her rouge cheeks and colored lips had turned her soft face doll-like. She had never seen herself look so fashionable or... beautiful.

She reached into the high collar of her shirt to draw out her familiar cross necklace, but her fingertips only found bare skin. Fear tightened her throat as she groped around her neck.

"Mother's necklace," she breathed into the quiet room.

When had she worn it last? She wore it into the ball, even if Edith claimed it was too plain and stiff to wear to a party. But had she still worn it while she undressed in the darkness of her room? Evelyn rose from the vanity to search the floor, but her frenzied search under the furnishings proved it was nowhere to be found.

She sat back on her heels with a groan. She must have lost it somewhere between the estate ballroom and her bedroom. Several miles and hours stretched between the two.

She swallowed as she leaned against the bed. Was this her punishment from God for going against her stepmother? The loss of her own mother's necklace felt too cruel, especially considering that this was her first infraction.

"Evelyn!" A shrill call cut through her closed bedroom door.

Evelyn buried her face in her hands, knowing without being told she was late for assisting the housekeeper with breakfast. As she stood to her feet, she gathered her emotions to tuck them away behind a complaisant veil. Descending the two flights of stairs to the ground level of their narrow townhouse, she tried to erase all thoughts of the night from her mind. Upon reaching the base of the stairs, she straightened her shoulders under her stepmother's impatient gaze.

Prudence stood with her fists planted on her corset-narrowed waist. Even if it was several years behind the current style, her blue dress with black ruffled trim and leg-of-mutton sleeves made her look every bit their middle-class status, if not a bit more.

"Lottie has been preparing breakfast on her own," Prudence snapped with a lift of her chin. "Where have you been?"

"I'm sorry. I overslept." Evelyn lowered her eyes. If the housekeeper was in such desperate need of help, where were Dahlia and Florence? "I'll help her finish."

Evelyn made her way through the dining room toward the kitchen. Both of her stepsisters sat at their places on one side of the dining table, their steely gazes trailing her as she passed through. In the kitchen, she found Lottie dishing cream of wheat into four porcelain bowls.

"I'm sorry for oversleeping." Evelyn grabbed the tray of jams and fixings already prepared.

"I'd oversleep too if I climbed to my room well after midnight," Lottie muttered under her breath without pausing the wooden spoon in her hand.

Evelyn froze, pressing the tray into her stomach. "Do you think anyone else heard?"

Lottie pursed her lips as she carried the bowls to the dining room. Evelyn followed behind the housekeeper with the tray, her cheeks warming. Neither woman said anything as they set the food before Evelyn's stepfamily.

Dahlia sniffed as she looked down at her bowl. "Cream of wheat? Father got eggs."

"This will fill out your bones just the same." Lottie kept her words light enough to not offend, but a firm undertone discouraged argument. "I have linens to wash. Excuse me."

Prudence frowned at Lottie, but the housekeeper disappeared before Dahlia could complain further. Evelyn slid into the seat next to her stepmother and began to top her cream of wheat in silence. As she flicked a glob of jelly off the spoon into her bowl, her mind couldn't help going to the arrangement of pastries and finger foods offered at the party. Daniel had selected a plate of options to share as an intermission to their dancing, asking if he met her tastes with his choices. She would have eaten cod liver oil if he had offered it.

She was unaware of the smile lifting her lips until her stepsister gave an indignant sniff.

"Someone is in a good mood," Florence commented as she picked up her spoon, but her glowering gaze caused Evelyn to tense. "And here I was assuming you were late to breakfast because you were sulking in your room over missing that ball you begged all week for." She lifted one delicate eyebrow. The frizzy, auburn curls that framed her haughty face had fallen from her floppy attempt at a loose Gibson girl pompadour style.

Evelyn held her gaze, trying to decide if she knew something or if she was simply baiting her. Deciding to err on the side of caution, she turned her focus to her stepmother. "Where is Papa?"

"He's already at work. You would have known that if you were up earlier." Prudence didn't spare Evelyn a glance as she sprinkled brown sugar into her bowl.

How long did Prudence plan to hold that over her head? Giving up on conversation, Evelyn focused on stirring her cream of wheat. No matter how hard she tried not to, her mind returned to the events of last night. Nothing could seem to dim the warmth that spread in her with one thought of Daniel. The memory of his smile evaporated any of her displeasure.

Breakfast continued in a quiet fashion, with her stepfamily occasionally commenting on the day's plans to each other. As always, they intentionally left Evelyn out of the conversation, allowing her to remain blissfully in her thoughts and memories.

As Dahlia laid her napkin next to her empty bowl and politely excused herself, Evelyn glanced at her half-full bowl that she had been stirring more than eating.

Prudence stared down her narrow nose at Evelyn's food. "Are you going to let food go to waste?"

Before Evelyn could formulate a reply, the stairs creaked. Her heart leaped into her throat as she rose from the table and dashed down the hall.

"Dahlia?" She called up to the second floor, hoping and praying her stepsister hadn't gone any higher.

"I knew it!" Dahlia shrieked from the third floor.

"Leave my things alone!" Evelyn grabbed her skirt to take the stairs two at a time, but it was too late.

Dahlia came out of the attic room, the ballgown in her hands.

"You dug in my trunk." Evelyn clenched her fists.

"Where did you get this?" Dahlia shook the dress at Evelyn. "You can't afford anything like this. That rotten friend of yours gave it to you and took you to the ball."

"Give it back!" Evelyn reached in vain for the dress as Dahlia snatched it away.

"What is the meaning of all this noise?" Prudence barked from the ground-floor hall.

Evelyn lowered her head, hiding her shaking fists within the folds of her skirt.

"Evelyn defied your authority." Dahlia raised the dress as evidence for Prudence to see. "I found this in her room."

"Please give it back to me." Evelyn kept her voice even and quiet. "It's Edith's dress, and I can't repay her if it's ruined."

"I have half a mind to tear it up for your insolence," Dahlia hissed.

"Give her the dress."

Evelyn jumped at her stepmother's voice, and she turned to find Prudence now standing on the second floor with them. Prudence's thin lips were drawn in a taunt line, her eyes like bone-chilling ice.

Dahlia frowned. "But Mother—"

"We don't damage other people's property we aren't prepared to pay for," Prudence stated without a change in expression.

Evelyn swallowed as Dahlia shoved the dress into her arms.

"But she—" Dahlia whined until a raised hand from her mother cut her off.

"Did you go to the party, Evelyn?" Prudence asked.

Evelyn lowered her gaze. "Yes, ma'am."

Prudence's hand slapped across Evelyn's face. Still gripping the dress in one hand, Evelyn stumbled back a step and put her other hand to her stinging cheek. She turned a gaping expression to her unmoved stepmother.

"That's for your disobedience," Prudence spoke with a steely tone unchanged from before. "You knew my orders."

Evelyn swallowed down mounting frustration. "I don't understand why you said no to begin with. The outfit cost you nothing. We had no other plans. Edith picked me up. Edith did everything, and it was her invitation. It was a harmless, fun night." As Prudence narrowed her eyes, Evelyn rushed on, "I never disobey you. I always do whatever you ask. Why couldn't I have one night for myself?"

Prudence grabbed her arm, causing her to wince. "Because I'm your mother, and I told you not to go."

"You're not my mother."

This time she expected—and was prepared for—the slap to the same cheek. Tears burned her eyes despite her attempts to hold them at bay.

"Your father chose me as the woman of this house, and whether you like it or not, what I say will be the final word as long as you are under this roof," Prudence hissed. "I don't need a reason for my orders."

"But there was nothing wrong with it!"

"Nothing wrong?" She let out a bark of a laugh. "Girls like you don't belong at such affairs. Do you think one rich friend makes you an expert? Masquerading in a world where you don't belong will do nothing for you but fill your head with useless fantasies."

Evelyn kept her gaze on the hallway rug. Rebuttals filtered through her mind, but no doubt Prudence would have a quick answer for anything she said.

Prudence leaned closer. "What happens if a rich man decides to seduce you and have his way with you for sport?" Her whispered words left a chill down Evelyn's spine. She tried to pull away, but Prudence grabbed her arm again. "You're naive, Evelyn. You would believe every word coming off his honey lips and go along with it, ruining yourself forever. Humiliating your father's good name."

Evelyn closed her eyes as she turned her face away from her stepmother.

Prudence released her arm before whirling away, her skirts flaring and rustling. "Your father will hear about this the second he returns this evening. In the meantime, I'll inform Lottie you will clean up breakfast."

As Prudence stomped down the stairs, followed by a smug Dahlia, Evelyn hugged the satin dress to her chest. Her fingertips brushed her lips, and the feeling of Daniel's stolen kiss flashed through her memory again, sending a blanket of shame to smother the warm feelings from before. Had she almost fallen for an ill-intended seduction? Maybe she should thank the Lord that Edith rushed her home before anything more could take place in the garden.

Feeling numb except for the stinging in her cheek, she trudged up the steps to her room to return the dress to the trunk.

On her way back to the dining room, she passed Florence in the hall. Even if Florence had managed to stay out of the hallway drama, she didn't miss the opportunity to watch Evelyn's defeated walk with a faint sneer. Lottie met her with a sympathetic look before leaving the kitchen.

In the kitchen alone, Evelyn took a few even breaths before gathering the dirtied dishes, and she scraped what remained of her uneaten breakfast into the garbage bucket.

As she washed the dishes, her stomach knotted itself in so many twists she feared she would be sick. Had she narrowly avoided entangling herself in something compromising with Daniel? Were his intentions throughout the dreamlike night far different than she imagined? No matter how hard she tried, she couldn't believe it.

No matter what she envisioned, she couldn't make herself regret going to the party. Maybe that was even more reason for her to feel ashamed, but it was the best night of her life. How could she regret it?

"Honour thy father and thy mother."

The words taught to her since childhood echoed through her mind like an unwanted reminder. Perhaps she was in the wrong for not feeling ashamed for disobeying her stepmother. Her fingers went to her throat in search of the cross necklace, only to remember she'd lost it. Instead, she clasped her hands against her chest.

Lord, please forgive me for my dishonesty and disobedience. I won't let it happen again.

As she plunged her hands into soapy dishwater, she blew out a breath. The night before had been a wonderful, breathtaking dream, but it had been just that, a momentary dream. For years growing up, she had been infatuated with Daniel, and at least for a moment, she felt what it was like to be in his arms, whether his intentions for the night had been pure or not.

In the end, nothing happened. Now she had returned to reality, and nothing was more real than washing her stepfamily's dishes.

As she stacked the bowls and utensils in their appropriate cupboards, Evelyn had to admit to herself that maybe Prudence was right to a point: Daniel's world of glamor and money was out of her reach. She looked down at the front of her skirt and shirt riddled with water stains, and she tried to picture Daniel at her side in all of his finery. It was an impossible image to conjure.

"Evelyn! Are you about done yet?" Prudence's shrill call drifted from somewhere else in the house.

Evelyn closed her eyes and leaned on the kitchen counter. Daniel's world was outside of her reach, but remaining under Prudence's thumb was not a place she wanted to be either. Maybe her time would be better spent finding someone who could sweep her away from this house. A husband who would provide for her needs with love and carry her far away from her stepfamily.

That was a dream she was willing to forget Daniel for.

ABOUT THE AUTHOR

Megan Miles's biggest passion centers around creating character-driven historical fiction with themes reflecting God's grace. After penning her first story at nine-years-old, writing became an unstoppable habit that has filled her free time and her dreams ever since. When she isn't writing or working, she has a tendency to volley between every hobby under the sun, including reading, sewing, growing succulents, and playing with her dog.

For more information about her books and to stay updated with the latest news through her newsletter, visit meganmile sauthor.com.

facebook.com/mmiles.writer
instagram.com/mmiles.author